Helen Mae Innes grew up in Wainuiomata and has lived in Eastbourne, Kelburn, Newtown, Ascot Park, Iwataki, Dong Ying, Wimbledon, Meanwood, Smethwick, Rathmines, Gloucester, Karori, Naenae, and on a boat, in a yurt, and would like to live up a tree. She has travelled through 30 countries, mostly by train, and taught English in five countries to students from 100+ nations. After escaping her hometown and travelling the world she has returned to the people and the bush of her childhood. After completing her PhD in creative writing she has worked as an editor, copywriter, writing teacher, and writer.

First published by Piwaiwaka Press 2023
ISBN 978-1-7385926-1-6 (paperback)
Second edition published by Piwaiwaka Press 2024
ISBN 978-1-7385926-7-8 (paperback)
All rights reserved.

www.piwaiwakapress.org
Copyright © Helen Mae Innes 2024
Cover artwork: Chloe Stephenson
www.chloestephenson.com

This is a work of fiction. Unless otherwise indicated, all the names, characters, businesses, places, events and incidents in this book are either the product of the author's imagination or used in a fictitious manner. Any resemblance to actual persons, living or dead, or actual events is purely coincidental.

AND THE BIRDS
FLED TO THE BUSH

HELEN MAE INNES

Piwaiwaka
Press

Also by Helen Mae Innes

Fiction

Oracles & Miracles & Zombies

(with Stevan Eldred-Grigg)

Autofiction

Into the Woods: the healing power of birds

All the dead voices.

They make a noise like wings.

Like leaves.

Like sand.

Like leaves.

Samuel Beckett
Waiting for Godot

The leaves of the books are birds. The tightly scrunched ponytails of the girls are birds. The dreadlocks of their pothead boyfriends are birds. The doilies on the windowsills are birds. *The Dominion Post* held by an old man becomes a flock of birds and starts to fly away. The prescriptions for the sickness beneficiaries are birds caught in the downdraught. The white paper bags that recently carried raspberry cream donuts are birds. The receipts for reconditioned tyres are birds. The posters for a d-dub concert are birds. The *Jackson's Café and Burger Bar* wrappers, the *Dolla $ave* plastic bags, the *Awaawa Library Teen-Zone* fliers are birds.

The valley is calm, quiet, waiting. Mrs Henderson thinks it's earthquake weather, but she doesn't say anything, doesn't want to make a fuss. It's probably nothing. No one else notices it's quiet, too quiet, until everyone does at once, like at a party when everything goes silent, and no one wants to be the first to speak.

All the birds take flight at the sound of Mike's

motorbike backfiring. They lift, for a moment,
suspended.

    Everyone turns and stares.

      Will they fly?

        Will they soar?

          Will they scatter? Like confetti?

        Like polystyrene beans from a burst
beanbag?

       Or will they all move together as one?

       A rising,

          folding,

              sweeping,

                  blossoming,

               murmuration?

      All the birds are airborne,

       and the whole valley

         holds

          its

        breath.

A body loses twenty-one grams at the moment of death, and it's been conjectured that this is the weight of the soul.

Twenty-one grams less isn't a lot when you're trying to ship a body back from overseas even if they did give a discount for the drop in weight. It's still stupid expensive. When comparing costs, it's natural to start to question, *what's the point of shipping back a body instead of some ashes, they're dead, aren't they?* But we do it because it breaks our hearts not to. Or we don't do it and hold a small box of ashes in our hands, the same way Timothy, on this particular morning, stands holding a dead bird he's just found in the gutter. A kingfisher, a kōtare. We don't see them much around here. They like to eat frogs and baby eels and mud crabs, copper skinks, ornate skinks, grass skinks. Kingfishers usually like to hang out near the streams lower down the valley, not up here.

But even these birds get restless, want to branch out, explore new places, see the world. Well, when we say *see the world* what we really mean is *see another corner of the world*. For some of us, another corner of the world is London, or rather a corner of London – an underground station in a suburb, another one in the city, some galleries, museums, and a pub or club or two or three. In the case of the kingfisher, *see the world* meant see the other end of the valley – a small stream feeding into the main river, kōwhai rather than kānuka growing on the verges, a phoenix palm or two, maybe even a nīkau, or the birdbath in Mrs Henderson's garden perhaps.

Dangerous business that. Can end up dead.

The kingfisher, on its first trip across the valley hit the dining room window of Mr Henderson's house and fell dead to the ground. As if its death is not heart-breaking enough, it was then carried by Susan's cat Ashford out of the gate, down Kōwhai Grove to just outside Ryan and Jessica's fence where Defor dog barked, frightening Ashford, who dropped the kingfisher and has fled up the phoenix palm.

We can see Susan standing under the palm now, her face showing disgust, not only because her cat is now stuck, but because he's stuck in a phoenix palm full of sparrows and starlings – that is, pest birds. A phoenix palm is the indoor-plastic-ball-pit-horror equivalent in nature. It's the trampoline park of the avian world. It's NOISE and chaos and birds suddenly pecking at the eyes of another bird and screaming laughter that could easily be an axe-murderer or Marie on hearing the local gossip. It's all too much and it's joyous and horrendous and over the top and to Susan it's disgusting.

Defor dog's barking has resulted in half the inhabitants of the street coming out to offer advice or encouragement to Susan – not that she will ever accept either – and offer tasty titbits to Ashford – who rarely refuses. Fitu presents Ashford with a prime cut of venison, much to the disgust of Sia, who's been looking forward to it for her tea.

Timothy doesn't notice the cat up the tree just as the cat hadn't previously noticed the dog and the bird hadn't noticed the windowpane. What Timothy does notice is the dead copper skink still lodged in the kingfisher's beak, with the morning sun reflecting off its skin like a miniature sunrise. What a waste. The grief he feels over the death of the kingfisher is soon engulfed in a greater grief for a skink whose death hasn't even helped with the circle of life by becoming lunch.

And we all sigh, in our own way, at this realisation. A rustle of the wind in the rhododendrons, the conifers, a whispering of voices, a cooling of the air.

In a way it's unfortunate that the cat wasn't eaten by the dog and the dog then hit by a car – the tragedy would perhaps have become comical then. A bit of gallows humour to lighten the mood? But there are no cars running, not in that street, not anymore, and until Defor started barking a moment ago no one had been awake to see the tragic performance pan out.

The kingfisher is lighter than Timothy thought it would be, but the soul of a bird would weigh much less than the soul of a person and therefore the difference in weight between a live and dead bird would probably be imperceptible. So, the departure of the soul probably hasn't caused Tim's miscalculation. Does Timothy feel the loss of a soul as a loss in weight? He knows a rifleman weighs only six grams, because a rifleman – being New Zealand's smallest bird – has had its weight recorded to be marvelled at. Therefore, a bird's soul would perhaps only be perceived by the most delicate of scales.

And then a kingfisher would weigh, what? Twenty

grams? But a kingfisher – not being the smallest, the heaviest, the anything-est – means that no book ever thinks to tell you how much a kingfisher weighs, let alone how much its soul weighs.

But that's our preoccupation, not Timothy's. We should be concerned with more practical, pragmatic, paltry concerns. Susan's still muttering about Defor chasing her cat; Mr Henderson notices, glancing over the rim of his cup of tea, the smudge on his window; and Jessica's fuming at how early it is to have been woken up. A kererū flying into a window leaves a beautiful, albeit sad, *glass angel* – the feather dust leaving an imprint, like a fingerprint, a ghostly shadow, on the glass. However, a kingfisher – being smaller, lighter – leaves more of a smudge than an angel. Which is just as well, as it leaves Mr Henderson annoyed at the smudge but unaware of, and therefore protected from, the knowledge that a bird off to see the world has died by smashing into his windowpane.

The problem with finding a wild bird dead at your doorstep, or your pet cat or dog flattened on the road, or your budgie at the bottom of its cage, is what to do with the impulse to have a little funeral. Should we put it in a shoe box? Wrap it in a silk handkerchief? Do we wear black? Which music is appropriate? Or do we ignore it, forget, move on?

Hard to know. Leaving it under a bush is a possibility as flies can land on it, maggots can grow, flesh can rot down, bones can fertilise the soil for years to come. Why buy blood and bone from the garden centre for forty dollars a pop when you can leave your dead pet under the very bush it loved to sit under in the sun? It's natural. You can glance over at the pile of bones and skin and fur as you walk down the path to get the mail and see how poor old Fido's getting on. Down to the bones yet? Nope, still loads of maggots writhing away like it's a foam dance party.

But we generally don't like the smell, the look, the idea, do we? Well, at least not for people, loved ones, neighbours, friends, even unidentified strangers. So, we fill the bodies with chemicals, dress them up in fancy clothes and stick them in boxes made of dead trees. Some of us don't like doing that though. The irony of popping a recently vibrant, alive body into the body of a recently vibrant, alive tree is not lost on some.

Timothy pops the skink, the bird, the pair in his pocket.

Ahhh, Timothy. Timothy, Timothy, Timothy. Tim, Timmy, Tim-Tam, Tim-Tom-Tam-Bam. That weirdo, gaybo, bird-obsessed freakazoid.

Who?

It depends on who's talking to him. Or about him. Many have never actually spoken to him. Yelled at, talked at, talked about, sure. Men in uniforms, in suits, with clipboards, with notebooks, call him Timothy R. Grey, and those he went to school with call him, if they call him anything repeatable, just plain old Timster. Don't let the names fool you, he's an adult now, a young adult at that uncomfortable age of not a teenager anymore but still being asked what he'll do when he grows up. He's the kind of person who people still pat on the head or talk down to. Not necessarily in a bad way. Bouncers used to ask him for ID because they were just doing their jobs. The girls, the women, the old ladies are the only ones to call him Timmy and pat him on the head like a dog who pisses on the carpet, but who you can't bear to put down. Let's just refer to him as Tim from now on. That's what he prefers.

It's early morning. The grey warblers are warming up by saying, 'Have you got it yet?' But it's unclear what *it* refers to, so Tim pats down his pockets, pausing on the path. 'Got you!' says a voice – maybe a grey warbler but more likely a tūī or a bell bird. The tūī have been baiting those around them lately, mimicking them, like a child does, like Tim can do, when he forgets that people don't like that.

Tim hurries towards the road.

The birds all laugh, and we all laugh too.

Tim is loved, tolerated, forgotten, ignored, laughed at, puzzled over. Although not in that order. Definitely not in that order. Some, Tim included, would be surprised to know that he *is* loved. Everyone should be loved first. But not all of us are that lucky. The cuckoo's chick never feels loved by its biological parents and never passes on love because you can't share something you don't have.

Do you remember reading about those experiments with monkeys? Tim read about them at the doctor's once. In the *National Geographic.* Or was it the *New Scientist* or the *Listener*? One of those, anyway. They took two baby monkeys and put one with a steel robot monkey covered in fake fur and the other one with just a cold steel robot monkey mother. The baby with the warm fur 'mother' grew up to raise her own babies reasonably well – not great admittedly, but got the job done. The baby with the cold steel mother grew up to drag her baby round by the ankle and battered its brains out.

Fucken psycho bitch!

Though, to be fair, it wasn't entirely her fault, eh?

Shouldn't have had fucken kids though!

Anyway, the point is, love's like really important.

Says who?

We do disagree, somewhat, on this point.

It's not true to say cuckoos never feel loved. That's a mistake. Once they've killed their stepbrothers and stepsisters by pushing them, eggs or chicks or both, out of the nest, they have all the attention of stepmum and stepdad grey warbler. A cuckoo doesn't get much cuddling or many bedtime stories since the adoptive parents are run ragged feeding a lumbering chick twice their size. But it *is* fed – which is a kind of love. And they don't peck it to death, or throw it out of the nest, like some would, just for looking different.

So, maybe there's hope.

But even with that love the chick will probably grow up to abandon its baby too. Patterns like that repeat in families. They say you need to break the cycle of abuse. But, you must admit, abandoning your baby is better than battering its brains out.

Tell that to the abandoned baby.

Well, we take what we can get sometimes.

When Tim was a baby, he was forgotten about, left at a party by his psycho mum who said she'd go back and pick him up the next day, but never did. So, we can forgive Tim for talking to himself as he walks up the street. He's passing the phoenix palm with the dog, the cat, the neighbours, the piece of venison wedged into a crack at the end of a broom handle shakenly hovering in front of Ashford.

'Look at that poor boy, talking to himself again,' says Mrs Henderson to no one in particular as she flutters the net curtains at number three.

Mr Henderson, in the house directly across the street, is rubbing at the smudge on the windowpane with his pyjama sleeve and not having much luck when he notices Tim walk by. He looks up and inadvertently locks eyes with Mrs Henderson. They notice each other at the same time, waver for a moment, before both sets of net curtains fall back into place – dropped like stale bread for the ducks.

It's early. Dawn chorus early. Henry Masters at

number ten is lying in bed. While Tim's out and about, with a front row seat to the show Henry lies in bed listening through a slightly ajar window. In the past he's always had to rush to work in the wee hours but now he marvels at how beautiful it is in this street. It's great, like the lively chatter and tuning up before a concert. He imagines all the birds as delightful people with glasses of bubbly laughing, chatting, mingling, before a big show in the town hall. A nice concert. Not one of those loud things with bass like a racing heartbeat, and alcohol served in bottles.

'The legendary maestro and leading conductor saunters onto the stage,' Henry drones in his deepest baritone.

He raises his hands over the quilt cover and starts conducting, his hands twitching like fantails. But they soon flutter down to his chest.

Something's not quite right.

The dawn chorus isn't a concert, it isn't the New Zealand Symphony Orchestra. It's more like the friendly chatter at a gallery opening, with a small ensemble in the corner. He smiles and hums a little.

'No. That's not right either.'

He drums his fingers. Pre-concert drinkies, or even

a barbeque would have some ebb and flow. Some raucous laughter from some frightful woman, some man who'd had too much to drink and who talks too loudly about his property investments. There's always one of those, even at the best of parties.

He crosses his arms across his chest and thrums his fingers on his collarbone. He knows he's heard this sort of thing somewhere before. 'Where *was* it?' he demands.

The Residents Association? Rate Payers Association? He stops moving his fingers and listens for a moment longer.

No. No, it's more like the recent Community Board Meetings. That's it! Noise without beauty. Like a coop full of bloody hens.

Just because it's natural doesn't mean it's lovely.

In fact, the dawn chorus can get really boring after a while. Birds *will* just drone on and on, if we let them. They don't stop.

Henry should have made more of an effort to meet his neighbours over the years. This particular morning the teenage tūī are trying to get the third and fourth notes of their latest hit (or is it a taunt?) worked out. Something like, *yak yak yak, kōkako*. Not everyone appreciates their talents or efforts. Susan Harris wakes up every morning and throws a shoe or two into the bush at the back of the house and screams, *shut the fuck up!* Henry had always assumed, before having more time on his hands, that it was some sort of domestic.

But it's not. It's just Susan. Her screaming has no effect on the birds nor their singing, but we must assume that as this is repeated each and every morning it makes her feel better.

Tim always flinches at the yelling of *shut up*. Every morning on his way past it's *shut up* or *eff off* or some such phrase. Automatically he rolls his shoulders forwards up around his neck till his chin touches his chest when verbal insults fly over his head. But even hunched he's still somehow over six foot. No one's quite sure how tall he is because no one ever measured him. But Mike's five eleven and he has to look up so if anyone wondered they might guess at six two or three.

It's not clear if anyone has ever wondered.

Tim, despite his height, looks small, insubstantial. If he had a driver's licence, he'd have needed to know his height. But to get a driver's licence you need a birth certificate and who's got one of those?

Oh, *you* do? Lucky you. Lots of people do, or did,

it's true. But some don't, you know. Some like Tim.

Susan's not at home this particular morning to yell at the birds in the bush since she's trying to retrieve her cat from the palm in her front garden. So, the local starlings yell for her.

It's eff this and eff that. Bleedings and bloodys all over the place.

It's hard to say if a bird swearing is better or worse than a person swearing. The locals love the sounds of the kākā from the local sanctuary when they fly overhead, little understanding that the *natural calls* are the result of a ranger in Auckland teaching a couple of birds to wolf whistle some years back. When those two rapscallions arrived down here, they taught the local birds who in turn mangled the calls with their local accents resulting in the screeches that now pass for *charming characteristic calls*. But it's clear that the unnatural sounds of the kākā are preferred to the natural sounds of the starlings in the palm.

Soon Tim's at the end of the street where the track goes up into the bush. He turns and looks at the valley. Mrs Henderson has noticed this habit of Tim's and likes to think of it as a fond farewell. Marie would say, a bitter-sweet farewell. Derek Hope would say, who are we talking about again?

But, Doris, who's often a little surprised, though not unhappy, when she wakes in the morning recognises the look. It's the look someone gives when they're given the all-clear for cancer. She had wanted to say, *jolly well sod off, and good riddance!* Though, that's not allowed. She's encouraged to pin a little coloured ribbon to her blouse and smile and talk about being grateful, if she talks about it at all, even though she knows it'll be back.

She just knows it.

I might get a few good years in; she'd thought at the time. Might not. Long, short, years, months, doesn't matter. It'll be back. Might as well get used to the idea and not live in cloud cuckoo land. You've got to take the good with the bad, as Marie says, or, the fucked with the well and truly fucked up, as Mike says.

It's that look.

No one notices the starling in Tim's breast pocket pop its head out and start singing *I Want to Break Free*.

Tim walks into the bush.

*

On the valley floor everyone remembers the earthquake at least several times a day. It's hard to forget the feeling of the earth, the planet, the great expanse of land that's your rock, your foundation, suddenly breathe, heave, shout, roar, and eventually sigh and be quiet once more. The reminders are all still there – the liquefaction acting like moats around houses, once castles, now wrecks, the broken windows, the doors ajar, chimneys now divorced from their houses snaking across lawns away from the walls they once loved.

But Kōwhai Grove, winding up the hill towards the bush, is not quite steep enough to have landslides and not low lying enough for the land to liquefy. The picket fences stand neatly, the roses are pruned, the letterboxes checked – just in case – and the cars are still polished and garaged.

Tim's hacked-at haircut – often done by grabbing a handful of hair and cutting across with pruning shears, kitchen scissors, nail scissors, a carving knife, whatever's at hand – doesn't stand out in the valley as being anything out of the ordinary. But in the neatness of Kōwhai Grove it's often noted, commented on, laughed at, pitied, reviled. His hair's a dull colour, like a dirt track, like hair that never sees the sun, with strands of that nondescript colour that can look green if the light isn't right.

Just like some say the sea's blue because it reflects the colour of the sky, some say his hair's green because it reflects the colour of the bush, which is where he can usually be found.

Or perhaps it's just mould?

Tim smells like the bush. Like lichen, beech leaves, birds. Not an unpleasant smell necessarily, if you're used to it, not at all like the unwashed semi-homeless, not like the seldom-washed bogan clothing, unwashed not out of a lack of personal hygiene but because washing causes the black fabric to fade (a local fashion faux pas).

There's no hint of stale sweat, soiling, semen. Nothing offensive, as such. More an earthy smell, an alive smell. Perhaps, if it were synthesised, bottled, and sold in the city, it would be advertised as being herbaceous-warm, haylike, tobaccolike, nutlike, with hints of cinnamon, sweet clover, freshly mown grass, tonka, coumarin.

But the twigs in his hair and clay on his boots attest to his having just come from the bush, not a bar or a barber's, leading people to say he smells like shit.

Which, technically, is unfair.

Marie sometimes says, *Into the shower with you young man!* even though Tim bathes in the river daily. But the solar showers Simon has rigged up – first for his flat, and then for the whole street, consisting of black polythene sheeting made into bags, filled with water, and hoisted up high in cradles – are a welcome change from the river. Not only for their warmth but the inclusion of soap Marie makes in great batches in her shed, scented with Mrs Henderson's lavender or Andira's calendula flowers.

So, Tim, walking up past lawns still kept in order, houses unscathed, does stand out, like a weed stands out if it dares to grow on Henry's lawn. For the non-gardeners a weed is merely another green leafy thing, so live and let live, but for many Tim's merely another black-jean-clad no-good good-for-nothing young man who needs a proper haircut and a job.

*

'For fuck's sake, hurry up, Tim.'

Mike is striding towards the top of the hill. The top

of *the hill* is like a stage door. No one enters or exits the valley by way of any other route. Never has. Not really. You could, of course. You could bushwhack your way out of here over any one of the hills. Or in. (There's a point. Although coming *in*to the valley is, theoretically, an option, locals always talk in terms of escape.) But *the* hill is the way to go.

You'd think that would warrant the hill having a name, or a name well-known, a name used. You'd be wrong.

It used to be inundated with cars, of course, cars crawling over the hill like ants on a coffee bun, thousands leaving the valley in the left lane in the mornings and returning in the right lane in the evenings. They say you could've had a picnic on the other side of the road from the slow-moving traffic and not have been bothered once. Not true, of course. But a comforting thought, nonetheless.

There aren't any cars crawling anywhere anymore. A lack of petrol and an abundance of landslides blocking the routes in, and therefore out, put paid to cars. Well, there are cars, but not moving cars. Car-corpses lie like flattened dead possums used to lie in the middle of the road. You don't really notice them, acknowledge them, think about them the way you would a live, moving one with shining eyes – a running possum with eyes like headlights, a running car with headlights like eyes. That's something people notice.

But, by now, even the nicest of houses with freshly cut grass, weeded flower beds, painted shutters, and a cleaned birdbath in the centre of the lawn, have the problem of *what to do with the car?* Some, like Richard, still polish the car on Sundays and keep it looking spotless. Perhaps they're ignoring the fact that cars are suddenly useless hunks of metal, or perhaps they're waiting for the day when the Hill Road opens again, and the petrol tankers rumble on down to vomit their contents into the underground storage tanks. They're perhaps the same people who keep checking their letterboxes for the cheque from the insurance companies, despite no posties, and despite no post.

Even Henry Masters still hasn't fixed his bathroom because the insurance company says it won't pay out if anything's tampered with before the inspectors have been. And he's a man, let's face it, who's used to disappointment and betrayal. Ask someone to tell you about his ex-business partner, his ex-wife, and the profits from his ex-firm sometime.

So even the nicest homes run the risk of looking like trash, with rows of rusting cars along the streets.

Marie had a clever idea. She seeded the car seats with rata seeds, with clematis seeds, and the vines grew up and out the windows and around the frames giving some of the birds nice places to nest. They're like raised gardens adorning the streets.

But there was a Committee Meeting about that. Banned it was. A total disgrace. It's rumoured that Marie has started making seed bombs and lobs them through open windows of cars, of houses, of garden sheds, when out on one of her walks.

However, nothing has been proven.

But we were talking about the hill, weren't we? That's where Mike and Tim are. Sitting now. Waiting. The hill summit's a good place to do sitting and waiting. There are no cars, so people can, and sometimes do, walk up the road with a basket or a backpack full of food, and have a picnic with a view of the harbour, of Hill Valley, with their backs momentarily to Awaawa.

Or just beers. Beers are good. If you can get them.

For those who can remember, the hill used to

symbolise coming and going, leaving and staying, escaping and being trapped. It was a barrier, a border, a boundary. Something to be scaled. Later it became not a barrier to be overcome, but a sheltering force, symbolic of their salvation. The peak became a place of sitting, waiting, remembrance. The Hill Road's static now, not unlike how an animal hit by a car is static. Maybe stunned. Maybe dead. Worth checking at least.

When a bird hits a window, it lies in the grass not moving for a moment. Maybe stunned. Maybe dead. Maybe about to fly away.

The hill summit's up above it all. Above the mist that sits in Awaawa Valley sometimes until midday in the winter. Above the smell of the cow shit and piss seeping down the Hill River in Hill Valley next door. The summit is above the carless, houseless people who remain. Above the broken sewers, fallen houses, fallen women, and broken men. You can sit up there, in the sun, in the southerly, at the top of the world as far as you're concerned. You can pretend nothing has happened. Or nothing ever will. And wait.

Mike isn't particularly good at waiting. He's the kind who's often doing, running, talking, but not often waiting. He created the first roadblock to stop looters and was on the first border patrol to stop officials. But this is the summit. There's not a lot to do but chew grass, lie back, think, *fuck me I'm bored.*

Tim's supposed to be waiting too, but Tim doesn't know that waiting on the summit of the hill is the most-boring-fucken-thing-imaginable. Tim's watching native wasps fly out of holes in the clay bank. He's trying to guess which hole a wasp will fly out of or into next. It's very interesting.

It's actually a very fucken boring thing to do. For fuck's sake Tim, have the good sense to sit down and be as bored as anyone else would be! But Tim's stooping, watching a section of the bank, then hopping a few steps, slowly, quietly. Stopping. Squatting. Staring. Watching as a wasp crawls out and flies towards the bracken and springing after it, keeping it in sight as he tears over the terrain not caring about the gorse or the blackberry ripping at his skin.

'Tim … Tim!'

Mike tips back his head and tells the heavens instead, 'Fuck! … Timothy!'

Tim loses sight of the wasp in the foreground and finds Mike directly behind it slowly coming into focus.

'What? What, what?'

'Sit the fuck down and act normal, will ya?'

Tim sits down exactly where he's standing. Most people look down, taking care not to sit on a sharp stone, or some shit, or something. Most people look. Not Tim. He's been told to sit and so he sits. A wasp flies out of a hole directly behind him and hovers above his head, just out of his line of sight.

Tim's excited. And confused. He's been given a task. He's seldom given a task. Being given a task requires first being noticed, being named, being recognised as having a skill that's needed. Tim's often told to just keep out of the bloody way. So, he usually just does his own thing and tries to avoid being beaten for no reason, or for no reason he can ever see.

Mike's been given a job to do too, and it worries him.

There's no wind. No southerly, no northerly. The gorse seeds crack and pop in the sun. It reminds Mike of the sound of breakfast cereal when you pour the milk on. Of the sound of another world, another lifetime. He's bored and that always pisses him off. Wanting to be angry, he starts throwing stones at the clay bank. Wanting to be really angry, to take that aggression out on something else. But he's also too bored to put any real effort into it.

Tim jumps up.

'Noooo!'

He starts stroking the lichen on the clay bank. Mike stops, a stone held high, ready to be unleashed.

'Ah crap, what's wrong with you now?'

'Wasps, wasps, you're hurting wasps.'

'Wasps? Wasps are wankers. Why are you bleating on about them?'

Tim picks up clumps of clay and tries reattaching them to the bank.

'Native wasps – our wasps are native. Native wasps don't sting, won't sting.'

Mike sinks back down and places the rock beside him.

'Sorry Timmy. Didn't know, eh. We've got native wasps, do we? Well, fuck me, I didn't know that. What are they called then?'

'More than two thousand, two, two, thousand, more than two thousand species of wasps. No book, no names. No names, no knowledge. I don't have no books and books know the names.'

'You don't know? Okay. Well, sorry. I didn't know either, eh.'

'Look! Look! They live in the clay, in the holes in the clay, in the clay in the bank, in the bank in the hill, in the clay in the holes.' Tim looks up at Mike like an excited kid. 'Scary? Not scary. Scary? Not scary. Don't be scared, Mike! Mike, don't be scared!'

It's the waiting perhaps. Or the lack of wind. Or the gorse seeds popping. Or the black wasps which Mike's never noticed before. Something doesn't feel natural.

Then Mike see him, a man walking up the western side of the hill. He has the stride of someone young, strong – that might be useful.

But he's not from here. Remember that Mikey. He's not from here.

'Come on Timmy, we're on.'

The two young men stand up and take a few paces forwards. Some of the wasps go with them, as backup perhaps, getting ready to flank the newcomer if necessary.

Mike doesn't notice.

The man is carrying a backpack larger than himself, with shining metal poles poking out. Tent poles, shovel handles, aluminium walking sticks which he's seemingly forgotten to use. Everything looks new, modern, sleek.

'Here we go,' says Mike.

They could walk down the hill to say hello, to shake hands, to offer to take his pack. But honestly, it doesn't occur to either of them, so let's not hold it against them. They were at the crest of the hill. Hardly anyone goes down into Hill Valley unless they have to, are compelled to. They're seldom mentioned, the reasons why, perhaps even seldom thought of. People just make excuses and allow others to make equally implausible excuses not to go into Hill Valley anymore. Where once they dreamed of escape many can't stomach the thought of leaving again.

So, the hill summit's where Tim and Mike stand waiting for Anton to climb the last forty metres.

Summit sounds high. It's not that high, just over a thousand feet. And yes, everyone does say feet and not metres because even if you're not going to claim the title *mountain*, you'll be damned if you're going to remember a number like 305 metres. So, yes, technically a mountain, under the old definition at least, but no one's going to call it that when every other peak on the ridge is more or less the same height. No one, that is, except poor old Anton who has never climbed anything so high in his life, and before landing on these shores had never seen anything so high. So, he might say it's the peak, the crest, the summit, the crown, the pinnacle. Those terms are all far too grand for a local to utter though. But it's the top, and it's well, no pun intended, it's all downhill from there. So, Mike and Tim stand at the top waiting, not thinking to go down even a foot or two in greeting.

Poor old Anton though, trudging up the slope, which is not really that steep, but his fitness is the fitness of a man from a city, a reasonably flat city, where he might sometimes take the lift up to a gym. Anton notices that these two men won't even take a step towards him so he's starting to feel apprehensive. He wants to stop and have another break but now they've seen him he feels compelled to slog on.

He had imagined being greeted further down and receiving offers to take his pack. He had resolved to say no. First impressions and all that. But the locals will be friendly, salt of the earth types who will insist. Won't they?

Though admittedly he'd been warned. The locals won't want you there, his supervisor had insisted. Not after everything they've been through. They're real troublemakers in Awaawa. They'd been losers before the earthquake but look at them now! Paranoid, belligerent, stubborn failures trying to create some new society, refusing to accept reality and move on. Only an idiot wouldn't accept the government resettlement plans up north. Fancy turning down a smart new townhouse full of all the modern conveniences! You'll have your work cut out for you there, among that lot, lots of people had said. Although, as no one with advice for Anton had ever been there, maybe it was even worse than they'd said?

Perhaps we should feel some pity for the young man? It had been a hot day, after all, the sweat had turned his hair a shade darker and his T-shirt was sticking uncomfortably to his chest, he'd just taken a boat across the harbour and fed the seagulls on the way, his supervisor expected ridiculous amounts of data in possibly hostile conditions, he'd have to spend his days searching for birds and his nights writing up results, and he still didn't know where he would stay in the valley. He'd heard all the houses had fallen down and he envisioned a tent city. He had a solar charger for his laptop, but the valley was infamous for its fog and there was the prospect of having to write up everything by hand. By hand!

We could feel pity for him, but we won't. He's come from comfort, from hot showers and hot meals, electric lighting, and motorised transport. But it's when he opens his mouth that we make up our minds: his consonants are enunciated, his vowels differentiated, his sentences grammatical. Who the fuck does he think he is?

'Michael? Timothy? It's so nice to finally meet you both. I'm really looking forward to working together.'

You see? Arsehole.

Mike stares at Anton the way you might look at a tree stump that needs removing. A large knotty tree stump. And then you remember you've lent your garden tools to a friend. After a long pause Mike speaks.

'I thought you were from Auckland. You're not from Auckland.'

'Ah, not so much Auckland as Auckland University. I have a scholarship with them to conduct research here. But, no, I'm from England originally, if that's what you mean.'

Mike kicks at the dirt with his boots, hands in pockets, thinking.

Anton doesn't know what to do, so keeps talking.

'Ripon actually, a small town, not unlike your own in many ways.'

Anton stumbles. While it's true Ripon has a similarly sized population, from what Anton had heard the two places had little in common.

Mike sniffs loudly.

'So, we were told to show you around.'

'Oh, well, that's ah, exceedingly kind of you. I should like to see my accommodation first if that's not too much trouble. I have rather a lot of equipment with me, as you can see. It'll be good to set it down, get settled in. That kind of thing. Long trip!'

He's talking too much, he knows it. He always talks too much when nervous.

Gorse seeds pop in the heat of the sun, the wasps hover for a second not knowing whether to attack, or retreat, or just carry on with their day. And Mike, who's been sent to meet this man but who was secretly eager for a new face, an extra pair of hands, falls silent in despair. The danger of letting in a university student was always that he'd be all mouth, too scrawny, too lanky, to lift anything, too much of a city boy to know his arse from his ammunition. But a Pom? What would he be able to do? Probably couldn't do fuck all.

Another one.

Mike spits on the clay track.

'What's it exactly you're doing here again?'

The welcome has turned into a challenge. The men blocking a path into the valley have turned into adversaries and Anton begins to fret, not about the physical challenge, the prospect of a fight, or of not gathering his data, but the possibility of having to fill in paperwork again. Paperwork for why the grant money hasn't been spent in the way he had anticipated spending it, paperwork for changes in plans, paperwork for new proposals, new grants, new deadlines.

Anton hates paperwork.

Travel the world, they said. Choose a topic that takes you to a tropical paradise. An island in the South Pacific. Ha! It was cold and damp, but at least he could be alone. All Anton wanted to do was go and sit in a forest where there was no paper, and no paperwork, no cross-cultural miscommunication, no uncomfortable silences. The two men are in his way, and he needs their help, and even, he just realises, hopes for their companionship.

He makes up his mind to start a charm offensive when he's distracted.

'Oh look,' says Anton as he points in Mike's direction. 'You have an ichneumonid wasp hovering over your left shoulder.'

Mike looks not where Anton's pointing but at Anton's finger, then looks Anton dead in the eyes and raises his eyebrows. Anton withdraws his finger into his hand, hiding the offending digit.

Why does he say that? Why is he such a *bloody noddy* sometimes? Afterall, no one cares about bugs. Say something that ingratiates you Anton, for Pete's sake!

Tim steps forward, smiling. Well, maybe not steps, more like skips. Tim, who rarely looks people in the eye or talks to them conversationally or greets or farewells, and always says the wrong thing at the wrong time, steps forward and grabs Anton's hand. Weakly, admittedly, but intensely all the same. He shakes it up and down, up and down.

Anton has noticed the wasp.

'People think wasps, think wasps, are enemies, our enemies,' says Tim. 'But they come, they come with us, with us, with us. They come with us.'

'Do they?'

'They do! They do!'

If anyone else had been there, Mike and that person would have shared a look. Shared a *what-the-fuck-is-going-on* look. A look lasting a fraction of a second but completely understood by both parties. A look almost anyone in the valley would have given or received and understood without needing to think about it. A language never learnt but one residing in the bones, the guts, the fingernails.

But no one else is there and Tim and Anton share a look instead. A fumbling, grasping kind of look. Full of uncertainty and surprise because neither Tim nor Anton have ever had the feeling of looking into someone else's eyes and seeing something of themselves reflected before. Of seeing the shadow of an ichneumonid wasp and not flinching because each man knows that type of wasp won't attack. Anton, loving bugs more than birds, doesn't flinch. If not among friends, then he's at least not amongst enemies. Well, not all of them. But there was an opening for him here at least.

Mike has always straddled different worlds. He has a foot in each camp and an ear for understanding something of what others believe. A knack for finding common ground. But he's never been the odd one out before. He too recognises something in Anton. The mark of an outsider.

Tim's an outsider of course, but he was born here, raised here, brought up, slapped down, trampled underfoot, and survived growing up here. And still survives here. A local and yet somehow the local language is not one he's fluent in. He's known, and maybe not liked, not loved much, not understood by most, but known and tolerated, and perhaps has even earned his place by merely surviving. God loves a survivor.

But here, dripping sweat on the clay, is a stranger, a newcomer. Is he friend or foe? Weak or strong? Useful or useless? A troublemaker? A spy? Or just another city slicker dreaming of utopia who has to be fed and sheltered because he's too fucken useless to do those things for himself?

Mike could have written him off the moment he laid eyes on him. But he hesitates.

'You're here to count birds or something?'

'Well, yes, I'm collecting data—'

Mike waves away the rest of the sentence like he's

waving away a wasp.

'Thing is, what do we get out of it?' says Mike.

'Sorry?'

'Look, it's all very well having this little project of yours ...'

'It's a PhD actually.'

'Whatever, your little project, but what I want to know is what do we ...' Mike shows with a hand gesture that Tim and himself were the *we* and not Anton. 'What do *we* get for helping *you*?'

'Oh. I thought the Community Board had, well my understanding was, everything had been arranged, that is approved, for my research to proceed?'

Mike frowns. The sun's directly overhead making it too hot to stand around gasbagging.

'They did, yeah. But we're the ones trudging up here when we've got better things to do. We're the ones who'll be showing you around, giving you shelter, finding you food. Well, for a day ... or two ... perhaps. You do know there's a shortage of housing here still? The government keeps knocking down perfectly good houses, saying they're too damaged for us to live in, trying to get us out. Then you come and want a bed. What do we get out of it? Can you hunt, can you fish? Can you grow food. Can you build? Can you support yourself or anyone else?'

'Hunting?' Anton involuntarily makes a face. 'Ah, no, I ah, never, well I've never been hunting.'

'Did you bring any food?' Mike nods at the pack that Anton's secretly proud of carrying but looks on the small side to Mike. 'Enough for your whole stay or do we have to feed you too? And for what? So, you can listen to bloody birds?'

Anton shifts his feet uncomfortably. They hurt from the walk up the steep hill and he's still feeling queasy from the boat ride across the harbour. Queasy from seasickness and queasy from the thought of the tsunami that swept up the river delta behind him after the *big one*. Even though they say the size of the tsunami was a once-in-a-thousand-years event his stomach won't listen to statistics. He wants to get over the crest of the hill into the safety of the valley, to see the infamous community that refused to leave after the city-wide evacuation of the remaining survivors. He wants to escape into the dense bush surrounding the community and listen for bird calls.

Tim turns and looks at Mike. Actually, looks him in the eyes. Eye contact with two people in one day, in one week even!

'He saw the wasp, Mike! Saw the wasp! Wasp, wasp, wasp, wasp, wasp.' Tim repeats the same word over and over, mimicking the sound the insects' wings make when flying.

If anyone else said such a thing Mike might punch them or at least swear, a stinging-nettle-in-the-eyes string of swearwords at such a ridiculous statement. But this is Mike, big tough Mike who can punch and kick and humiliate as well as the next man and weird Tim, who's like an old teddy, dragged through the mud, sat on, thrown around, but then sewn up again. Loved and yet not loved. Loved, but so subtly few recognise it as love.

So, he lets Anton into the valley not because of the Board's approval or the robust grant application or the polite tone of voice the newcomer always uses with strangers even when it makes him sound like a dick. Mike lets Anton into the valley because of a wasp.

A wasp can be as good a reason as any other. Bugs were the reason Anton studied zoology in the first place. He'd had an extensive ant farm as a child, then moved onto crickets and wasps. However, birds, not bugs, get grants. Especially here. So, birds have brought him to the valley, but bugs now let him in.

'Oh, fuck it,' says Mike. 'Okay, Tim?'

'Yeah? Yeah, yeah?'

'You show Anton around, okay?' He vaguely waves a hand across the ridge to the south.

Anton looks in that direction, at the unremarkable regenerating bush and scrub, not the habitat he needs to explore at all. Mike's standing on a perfectly good road, a bit cracked perhaps, but wide, sealed, and not covered in landslides like the road up. It clearly heads directly towards the township. Anton clears his throat.

'I thought, perhaps, I could get settled in, get started tomorrow? It's been a long day getting here.' He gestures back at the steep road into Hill Valley, to the flat valley floor bordering a flat harbour.

Mike flicks away a piece of grass he's been chewing.

'This here's Timmy. Timmy knows all the birds and bugs and trees in the bush. Feathers and nests, eggs, that kind of thing. You need something, you ask Timmy. He's going to show you the bush now.'

Mike turns to Tim, wide-eyed disbelieving Tim who was looking from Anton to Mike, Mike to Anton. He's never been introduced as an expert before. He doesn't remember being important enough to be introduced to anyone before.

'Tim, you listen to me. You take the Grawler Track alright? All the way along. Wait for me at Kererū Corner.'

'I could bring him, bring him down! I could—'

'No, you couldn't. I've got to go see a man about a dog.'

'Dog! We're getting a dog?'

'What? No. I'm going to see Pete, okay?'

'Pete's getting a dog? I like dogs. Dogs. I can help with dogs.'

Mike sighs. 'No one's getting a dog. Wait for me at Kererū Corner.'

'Wait for you, wait, wait at Kererū Corner, okay, corner the kererū, go to Kererū Corner.'

And he's off, Tim is striding along the track to the south. Long legs flicking out and around and finding themselves on the earth as if by accident and then flinging into the air again, one after the other at amazing speed.

Anton stares at Mike. He doesn't know where the Grawler Track leads, but it seems, by his reckoning, to be the long way around.

'Off you go. Timmy's off, and off you go too. You don't want to get lost now, do you?'

Mike turns and walks down the abandoned four lane road as Tim disappears around a bend in the narrow bush track. The wasps long since retreated to their holes. The gorse bushes are no longer firing their seeds into the air. The sun has moved around, and Anton's left in the shade.

A starling lands on the path and stares up at him. Anton wonders if he's suffering from sunstroke as he could swear the bird's singing *Keep Yourself Alive*.

*

You would think that Mozart having a starling as a pet would have given the practice some legitimacy, but this is Awaawa and Mozart is, is what? The name of the Greek guy who runs the chippie down Queen Street? The name of one of those expensive make-your-baby-smart musical programmes that always end up in the free cardboard box outside the op-shop? Phoebe learnt the flute at school and wanted Mozart pieces to play, but was told *children don't like classical music* and was given 1950s rock and roll classics. Not given even one

Jethro Tull flute solo. No. The local music teachers had heard of Mozart, sure, but assured Phoebe she wouldn't like him. Maybe it was because there had been that movie which made him look like a bit of a pervert? Who knows?

When Tim saw a nest dropping from a tree, he showed a dexterity that no one knew he had, flying through the air himself landing hard on his right shoulder, arm stretched out, nest intact and cushioned in his outstretched palm. It was the first experience of flying for both the chick and for Tim.

The starling was an only child. Unusual for a starling. It used to be unusual for people in the valley too. *Lonely onlys* they called them. But then times changed and only children were all the rage. Or were the thing. The norm. Perhaps most people have one child in them the way they say most people have one book in them? Older parents, older sperm, older eggs. The body saying, *do that again? You've got to be kidding!* and shutting up shop. Or maybe it became too expensive, or there wasn't enough time in between paying the mortgage and endlessly scrolling through social media.

Would we describe Tim as being an only child?

Does he have siblings, left behind at parties all over the country? Or could you describe all the other kids who've been raised by Mr and Mrs Grey as siblings? Tim's not alone, in the sense that he grew up in a house full of people. But does anyone look like him, sound like him, act like him? Would you say those two fell from the same tree? Not if you looked through one of the three bedrooms. Not if you looked at the piles of blankets and kids on the couches. Not if you looked in the fort that was built under the kitchen table that somehow became the bedroom for one of the children who eventually grew so big their legs stuck out the end under one of the chairs. Not if you looked in the bed in the *fourth bedroom* – the barricaded off and repurposed bit of hall leading to the front door. You wouldn't find anyone like Tim in the foster home, the flat, the street, the valley.

But if you open the back door, walk not around the house towards the road, but up the path, past the clothesline, the veggie garden, the dog kennel, the half fallen down glasshouse, the garden shed, the sleepout, the compost bin, the once prized treehouse … If you walk to the end and through the gate into the bush and trudge up the track to the ridge and stop at the top and listen, and breathe in deeply, and smell the black beech leaves decomposing, and the lemonwood flowering, and hear the low undertone of the crickets, the louder pitch of a few cicadas, the grey warbler in the distance, the korimako near your left shoulder, the kākā screeching overhead on their way up the valley, the tūī mimicking the korimako, feel the humidity in the undergrowth and hear the murmuring of the leaves above, the low squeak of the supplejack moving into crevices, the rocks expanding in the heat of the sun, feel an aftershock reaching your feet, see the colour of ferns where the rays reach through the space left by a recently fallen tree … If you feel that, see that, smell that, hear what the birds and the rocks and the wind and the leaves and clouds are telling you, then would you say Tim is an only child?

Tim tastes the bush in a way that others cannot understand. Some think, perhaps, the taste of the bush is an infusion of kawakawa tea, packaged in non-biodegradable teabags along with imported mint. For Tim, the taste of the bush is the taste of life, the act of licking the lips to prevent the skin cracking, without even being aware of it, and yet delighting in the simple act. Tim's so full of the bush that no tree ever wonders if Tim's an only child. Is a seedling ever an only tree?

Do you remember, before the concrete cracked and all sorts of plants pushed through like Boxing Day shoppers, how streets were neatly paved, and the only greenery was geometric? Squares of green were hemmed in, sprouting trees a child would draw, a trunk, a round bobbing ball of leaves. In their own way they were reminders of only children. Their proliferation, their replacement of rose bushes and beds of pansies with native bushes and grasses, confined within concrete *architectural planters* coincided with the popularity of only children in human society, though no correlation or causation should be inferred. The single trees in concrete squares every twenty metres down the centre of every pedestrianised street in the nation were reminders of only children. But worse, orphaned only children.

Once, when Tim used to sit in the university library all day, he read an article about how mother trees feed their children, how strong trees send nutrients to weak ones, how trees with light send nutrients to ones in shade. The researcher had used radioactive isotopes, injecting them into some trees and using Geiger counters to track where the isotopes went. The trees looked after one another. They communicated. The strong, the old, nurtured the others, the weaker, younger ones in the community.

Meaning we can't look at a tree and not see the forest. The tree *is* the forest. So, later that day when Tim walked from the uni down to the city centre and saw trees caged by concrete planters, spaced out in rows, with no earth connecting them, just neat, orderly paving-stone-lined pedestrian zones, he cried out. He saw orphaned trees, isolated from kin, isolated from any contact with their own species. Do trees get lonely? Depressed? Is solitary confinement as torturing to them as to us? Is a solitary tree in a concrete pit imprisoned? Is a planter box cruel and unusual punishment?

Dig your fingers into the earth. Do some gardening, or just sit under a tree and reach down to communicate. The *Mycobacterium vaccae* bacteria in soil is a natural antidepressant and it's cheaper than Prozac, and gardening is not seen as drug-seeking behaviour so no need to be on your guard trying to look normal. Gardening makes us happy, it's scientifically proven. (Though, if you are a spiteful, chainsaw-gripping type of gardener that may not apply. Does Henry with his hedge clippers, freshly sharpened, walking around trying to find something, anything, in need of cutting back, count as being a gardener?) It's conceivable that nurses who have read the same research walk around hospital wards with pots of dirt saying, pop your hand in there dear and we'll have your anxiety cured in no time.

Tim got a warning once, from a Community Patrol Officer, about leaving trails of dirt connecting one tree to another. What Tim had really wanted to do was find a sledgehammer and create ditches along the footpath. Rip up the whole street, or even the whole city! But instead, he merged back into the bush and the leaves of the trees embraced him.

Perhaps both Tim and Starlight are siblings of the bush. So, whether Tim's an only child or not is irrelevant. The starling named Starlight doesn't think about such questions. The starling whistles *Bohemian Rhapsody*, but only part of it, which always bothers Mike.

One time, as Mike and Tim walked down the track to the valley floor, Starlight flew from branch to branch singing the same line over and over.

Mike lost it. 'Why the fuck can't he ever finish the

verse?'

Tim tried to whistle the last couple of notes to complete the tune. He wasn't sure why Mike needed it but knew something of that feeling.

Starlight hopped along a branch saying, 'Whydafuck? Whydafuck? Argh, whydafuck?'

*

If there's one thing Derek Hope (Des to his friends) likes, it's welcoming fresh faces into the valley. Lots of lively young things have come in since, well you know, that day. Full of ideas they are. The young. Oh, to be young again, so fresh, so vibrant! Change the world, they will.

Derek combs his hair, loops his tie (he still wears a tie each day, no reason for standards to slip) and opens the front door. Maggie comes out of the greenhouse as he walks down the path.

'You off then love?' she says.

'Indeed. Things to do. That young man is expected today.'

'The university man?'

'The very one.'

'Who's guiding him in?'

'I sent Michael and Timothy.'

'Oh, do you think that was wise?'

Derek purses his lips. He's been voted mayor two terms running, and before that ran a successful little travel firm.

Maggie notices the line between his eyebrows deepen.

'It's just that, well that young man Timmy, he's a bit ...'

'Timothy? Well, yes. He's a bit ...' Derek taps his head with his forefinger. 'That's true, but he's into birds, isn't he? Crazy about them, if I recall correctly, so I thought they might get along. Be a nice spot of company. Don't want the new man getting lonely.'

'You don't think the university man will think poorly of us? We could do better than Timmy as a representative, couldn't we? Remember that television crew?'

Derek scowls and straightens his tie.

What should have been the crowning glory of his first term as mayor had been a nightmare. Thankfully, no locals had televisions anymore and the recording that was supposed to air in the park on the solar-run projector had mysteriously been lost in transit. He blamed the lack of postal services but had been required to pay Mike quite substantially to seek and destroy all incoming copies of the documentary about the valley.

But this university man. He will help to put the valley on the map again, so to speak. Derek has grand plans for Awaawa and the young man's just the man he needs. Derek always has a plan, but none's needed more so than now. It would work. It will work. And this university man's just the one to help. Derek just knows it.

*

Tim's got a headful of questions, but it takes quite some time and Anton tripping over yet another supplejack vine for the two men to stop and for Tim to ask one of them.

'You're a university man? A man of the university? A man of the universe?'

'Yes, that's correct. I completed my master's at Leeds University, then came to Auckland to do my PhD.'

Tim points in the direction where the local university once was.

'I loved university, universally loved.'

'Oh, *you* studied there?' Anton mentally chastises himself for sounding so incredulous.

'Yeah, yeah, well nah. Nah, nah, no. Yeah, I went there, there went I, there I read. I read the books; the books read me. I listened!' Tim holds his hands out like he's shushing Anton and looks around like a concert's about to start. 'I listened to lectures, to lecturers, to listen at the back of a lecture theatre, listening, liking, lurking in the library. Reading! Reading!' Tim laughs and shakes his head like an old man reminiscing.

Anton nods, not quite knowing what to make of any of what's being said, opens his pack and pulls out a bottle of water for want of something to do more than anything else.

'So, you weren't enrolled?'

Tim frowns then laughs.

'Fuck off, fuck off. Fuck! Fuck! Fuck off, would you?'

Anton's taken aback at the sudden insult, but Tim doesn't seem to have meant it as one.

'No money! Money! No money! No, no, no. But

they had books! Books on birds, books on books, books of shelves, lots of books, birds on books. Big books! This big! Big, big, big books!' Tim holds his hands apart showing the dimensions of the books he's read. 'I've seen them, I've seen them, I've seen, I've looked, I've spied, I found, I find.'

'Oh, well yes—'

Tim drops his voice and whispers conspiratorially. 'There was a little book, a tiny book, hidden at the back, in a nook, tiny, tiny, tītitipounamu, a bird with pounamu titties, a pocket guide, a guide for pockets, guide of pocket-sized birds, a bird in the pocket's worth one in the bush! The best book, book in a nook, their tiniest book, tiny tītitipounamu.'

'They let you issue books?'

'They did not!' Tim jumping up, suddenly shouting. 'I'm a student, I study, study books, study birds. A student of birds, making a study of song. "You're not," they said!' Tim freezes and looks around then squats and leans in close again. 'So, I took the book, the book of birds, bird book, and threw—' Tim swept his arm out violently like he was throwing a discus, almost hitting Anton in the chest. 'Threw the book … out the window! Out the window and it flew!'

Tim jumps up excitedly and flaps his arms. 'It flew, flying, not falling, fleeing! The librarians! Chasing me, chasing books, chasing birds. Out of the window.'

'So, you stole it?' says Anton before he can stop himself. He doesn't want to get on the wrong side of any of the locals, but it always irks him when library books aren't on the shelves when the catalogue says they are.

'No, no, no, no, no. I *freed* it.'

Anton tries to change the subject. 'What's your favourite bird then?' he says, cringing at how juvenile he sounds but not knowing quite what to make of Tim.

'Everyone likes tūī. Every one, every tūī. Tūī tūī tūī tūī, Tui likes tūī. But. I like bell bird, bird bells korimako, kori kori, makomako.'

'They're similar sounding, aren't they?'

'Listen,' Tim holds his finger up as though a bird's singing nearby and he's listening intently to its song. 'Korimako kori kori kori kori,' he wiggles his fingers gently like a miniature conductor's baton, 'Bell ... bell ... bird ... bird ... bell bird ... bird bell,' with each word he gently taps his fingers in the air. 'Beautiful,' he says gently. 'But, tūī?' he looks at Anton and then mimics rolling a cigarette and smoking it. 'Same tune, same song, same singing, same, same, but …' he mimes taking another drag again and pointing to the imaginary smoke making its way down to his voice box, before having a rather musical and yet also violent coughing fit, before he hawks, spits, and collapses in laughter.

Anton laughs. 'I hadn't thought of it that way,' he says. 'But I can hear it now.'

'And tīrairaka, piwaiwaka, pīwakawaka. Pi pi pi pi pi.' Tim spreads the fingers of one hand into the shape of a fan behind the other hand with fingers pointed to look like the body and beak of a bird.

Anton can hear the sound of the fantail cheeps in the clipped sounds Tim's making.

'Piwaiwaka are like people on P, eh?' says Tim as he adjusts his hands to watch the shapes their shadows make on the clay bank.

Anton doesn't feel qualified to comment.

'Look look look at them go go go!' cries Tim. 'Go piwaiwaka, go!'

Anton watches Tim mimicking the piwaiwaka flight not only with his hands but with his whole body. He wants to laugh but he's also jealous in a way, wishing he too could be so uninhibited. So free.

'Come on! Come on! Come on!' says Tim. 'Fly piwaiwaka. Piwaiwaka fly.'

Anton almost says no but there's no one else around. No one knows him here anyway. It's a fresh start. He forgets about his aching shoulders and worrying about where he's being led, jumps up and joins Tim, making another piwaiwaka with his own hands. The two of them, or six of them if you count the two shadow birds, two hand birds, as well as the two men, leap about, ducking, twitching, jerking, their hands making the piwaiwaka shadows flit over the clay, scaring native wasps back into their holes.

'What the fuck are you two morons doing?'

Mike stands on the path, legs apart with his arms crossed, an old supermarket bag threaded around one arm, frowning at the both of them. Anton's hands stop and drop, like a kererū hitting a windowpane. Tim's thumbs remain entwined but twitching gently like a bird rescued from the mouth of a cat. They both look down at their mud-covered shoes like naughty children.

'Thought you must've got lost. But no, you're prancing around like fucken lunatics. Come on. Time to meet the valley.'

When Tourism Awaawa had released tourist brochures that said the valley was an addiction many thought it was a bad joke. An addiction is something you can't live without, no matter how much you hate it, something you leave and never go back to if you can, or something you love and won't hear a bad word against, though deep down you know it's destroying you. It's not really a tourism catchphrase. Visit Awaawa and get addicted! We can guess that no one on the committee had a kid on P. Or maybe they did, and they were as oblivious to that as they were to the effect of their advertising slogans.

Awaawa is, or was, row upon row of wooden houses made of row upon row of horizontal weatherboards, spread throughout the valley. Back in the day, when all the windows were lit up at night, uncurtained or curtains undrawn, if you drove past fast enough in the mist the large plate glass windows looked like flickering TV screens, flitting by, one after the other, with mini flickering TV screens inside them. Flick, flick, flick, look through the car windows, though the lounge windows, through the TV screens at other worlds, imagine yourself somewhere else.

Mist is the wrong word. Or gives the wrong impression at least. Mist sounds airy and light and only a sunbeam away from not being there at all. But the mists in Awaawa are old lumpy duvets, mink blankets covered in snow leopards, dolphins, Siberian tigers, wolves howling at the moon. They lie where they fall. There's no settling. If you could drive through the mist and up the hill road there could well be sunlight and a magnificent morning well underway in Hill Valley. Mists burning off fences, off the roofs of houses in Naeroa, in Mitimiti, in Moeitera, in Waterton, in Worchester, in Woburn. While Awaawa sits like a forgotten child taken out of a bath, dripping, shivering on the sodden bathmat.

There was a time when all the nice, new suburbs had only English names, and then a time when all the nice, new suburbs had only Māori names. Swings, roundabouts, playgrounds, were named, renamed. A developer wanting to maximise profits might be tempted to name a suburb after a prominent person, a historic figure. Like Hill Valley, later Hill Valley City, named after Edmund Hill, the director of the New

Zealand Local Land Company Ltd. Most people seemingly having forgotten or never known that he was an unscrupulous bastard, ripping off both natives and settlers, and disappearing with a fortune to California. But few know the story. Outsiders often say something or other along the lines of, *What a stupid bloody name, is it a hill or a valley? Make up your minds!* But you can't blame the receiver of a name for its choice. Some say Timothy was named after a packet of Tim Tams his mum was eating when the midwife asked for a name, but that's probably just idle gossip.

*

As they walk, slide, and climb down a steep track into the valley Anton gets glimpses of the township through the bush.

'Is that Awaawa?'

Mike grunts.

'Not A-waaaaa-wa. It's pronounced A-wa-a-wa.'

'It's such a beautiful name. What does it mean?'

Mike takes a while to answer.

'Valley. Awa means valley.'

'And Awaawa?'

Mike can't help himself but tell the whole answer.

'My great-great grandfather's people were living

over the hill when developers arrived and started mapping out the place. Plots of land to sell. They asked him, "What's over there?" And he answered, "A valley." So, they named it Awa. Only, it wasn't its name, just what it was. And then later people added valley, so it became Awa Valley. But later still they thought having two languages together wasn't right, so they changed it to Awa awa, and then Awaawa.'

Tim starts singing quietly. 'Awa awa valley valley, valley Awa, Awa valley, dilly dally, silly Sally …'

Mike continues. 'Hill Valley, on the other hand, did have a name, a sacred name, but that's never acknowledged.'

Anton shuffled his feet. 'Ah, so what name should I use, to, well, to be respectful? Awaawa?'

Mike smiled. The name reminded him of his grandfather's laugh, of sitting with him listening to family stories before he died. 'Call it Awa Valley, Valley Awa, Valley Valley, Awaawa. I call it home.'

*

If you'd asked anyone about Awaawa back in the day everyone had an opinion. If the number of opinions matched the number of visitors who had ventured over the hill Tourism Awaawa would've been a happy committee of three. Ask someone to describe it, someone from *the right side of the hill* and they'll confidently tell you it's all State Houses (there are none), full of unemployed (lower rates than in Hill Valley) and full of crims (they're out-of-towners). Ask an old time local, say Derek Hope, and he'll tell you Awaawa had the highest rate of home ownership in New Zealand. Though of course he'll be thinking of the times before the housing 'boom' (or 'crisis' depending on the depth of your pockets) before the investors boasted about how the houses were cheap, but you could raise the rents so high you could make more of a profit there than in the *nicer* suburbs. Before they bulldozed the homes and put up tiny hovels dumped onto sections like a kid empties a box of blocks on the floor.

If you ask Richard, he'll tell you about the Olympic-sized swimming pool, the first in the region, financed locally from men dressing in their wives' ball gowns and taking turns being pushed in a wheelbarrow from door to door collecting donations. The same men later donning overalls to dig the hole for the pool, photographs of them looking sunburnt, filthy, and happy adorning the entranceway to the pool for years. Ask Richard's wife Annette about the early years and she'll tell you about the lack of a draper's store and having to get over the hill for cotton when some silly sod had gone and ruined the seams of her best dresses.

Derek Hope will tell you about the ten months when they were an independent borough but don't get him started on when they lost that independence again, swallowed up by the Hill Valley Council in the interests of getting enough residents to call themselves a city. And the locals will tell each other how they have the highest number of churches per capita and in the same breath say they also have the highest suicide rate in New Zealand. They don't mean to imply any relationship between the two statistics sitting side by side and no inference should be taken. Just as New Zealand having the highest number of flightless birds has no bearing on its also having the longest living eels. People just love boasting of being the first or the best at something, even if it's suicide, even if it's church-going and they themselves do not go to church. Not inferring causation or correlation between sentences uttered in the same breath was a skill Richard and Annette mastered in their marriage years ago.

For every hundred suddenly overpriced square wooden houses during the boom years there was a strip of three to five footpath-pressed terraced houses, repurposed from old fish and chip shops, hairdressers, dairies. Refurbished and sold as fancy apartments, their 1960's appearance suddenly looking new again. But who wants to live in a place smelling faintly of oil or hair dye and where the children can tap your windows and run away? Certainly not the locals who remember the original occupants, Marie, who used to cut as well as any other hairdresser but knew more than her fair share of gossip, and Andira, who ran the dairy and could count one cent lollies into a paper bag faster than the eye could see and was never wrong. How could anyone live in an apartment that had once been a butchers or beauticians? But they were often snapped up by first home buyers from Hill Valley, impressed by the new kitchens but also harbouring secret desires to save up enough to move on and thinking of the resell value of the double glazing.

Then later still the homes were bought up, knocked down, and where one home, one front lawn, one back garden, one veggie patch, one swing set had once been six townhouses would pop up overnight, like toadstools. The developers would buy up three neighbouring sections and fill them up like a careless bartender not looking where he was pouring.

The local shops, local schools, local kindys were all replaced over the years by larger, less friendly establishments found further away, and the local anything was then driven past. By Holdens, by Fords, by strong powerful cars. Outsiders thought those cars were chosen to inflate egos, but more than one adult had traumatic childhood memories of their mum's car being left at the side of the road and their having to walk up and over the hill to get back home. The shame! The memory of it twisting the guts into a knot, even now. Even Mike, tough old Mike shows something like a facial twitch at a certain bend. It's been noticed but as he didn't have a mother, she couldn't have broken down on the Hill Road so no one ever dares to ask him about it.

So, locals bought big cars. Good ones, with good tyres. Even after a bike and pedestrian path was built up the side and you could always pretend you were just out for an afternoon stroll or a power walk to get fit for the coming season, people bought good cars.

The community market's in full swing by the time Mike, Tim, and Anton get down into the valley. There've been rumours that a kissing booth's up and running and despite all the bravado even Mike's curious. But it was, Mike could now see, as almost all news in the valley was, mere hearsay, bullshit, lies. The Board have decided kissing booths are sexist, but instead of cancelling the tradition they've placed on the stool a young handsome man who looks as soft as marshmallow. Ashley-something-or-other, one of the newcomers. He's sitting and looking smug, though why he looks smug when there's no one lining up to kiss him Mike can't even begin to guess at.

A large man in shirt and tie, the only person Anton can see dressed like that, comes striding up to Anton, all smiles, and grabs his hand in a powerful handshake.

'Doctor Anton, isn't it? It is, isn't it? So, so nice to meet you!'

'I'm not actually a doctor, well not yet—'

'Welcome, welcome, Doctor. It's good to have your sort here in the valley again. Someone with a bit of smarts. After the earthquake, the bosses left, the managers, and lawyers, and accountants, and politicians, and bankers left. The suits left. The rest left on the planes north. The first thing the politicians did was fix the runway to get themselves and their friends out.'

Anton remembers having heard something similar in the news.

'Well, it's good to finally be here,' he says.

'Do you know,' continues Derek, 'that they didn't fix the main roads for the ambulances or fire engines? They fixed the runway and plane after plane flew away until there was no one left but us and we weren't going anywhere. There are still children who need teaching, and we're still here to teach them. There are elderly that need caring for and we care for them. The nurses, the fire fighters, the childcare workers, the rest home workers, the people who care for the rest of us are still here. The essential people who grow the food and prepare the food and serve the food are still here. We get hungry and we eat. We get sick and we are nursed back to health. We get bored and we are entertained.'

Anton's got the feeling Derek has given this speech many times before.

'The only thing that has left is the money and the

people who were helping to swish it around a bit while sucking it up. The parasites, the leeches have gone and left behind all the people who were doing all the work. The craft brewery's still open even though the CEO has left, and it runs all the better for it. The biscuit factory's still running even though the PR and HR lot have gone. We still make the biscuits, we still eat the biscuits, just the people skimming off the money have gone. So, we've done away with money altogether!'

Anton feels a stab of panic.

'But how on earth do you pay for things?' he says.

Derek laughs.

'Why do we need money? Do you need biscuits? Here, have a packet.'

'But I can't pay you.'

Derek forces the biscuits into Anton's hands and holds them there. Derek's giant calloused gardener's fingers grate against the back of Anton's hands. He looks Anton intently in the eye.

'What can you do? Who do you care for and how do you care for them?'

Anton swallows. Stares back, trying to think of what to say.

'He looks after birds,' says Mike.

'That's right!' says Derek. 'Birds! You look after the birds! Good, good. We're glad to have you here.' Derek nods.

'Well, yes, I suppose, in a way, you could call it that. However, to be perfectly honest, I'm more of an observer, a collector of data rather than a conservator.'

'Well, that's important, isn't it?' Derek slaps him on the back. 'We need birds, and the birds aren't going to pay you in money, are they? But it's all good. I have great plans for you my lad, but you go and get settled in. Plenty of time to talk about that later. You go and look after your birds. Do you need another packet of biscuits?'

Anton holds up his packet, like a baton. 'No, I'm all set, thanks very much.'

'We only have shortbread and gingernuts at the moment.' Derek shakes his head sadly looking down at the remaining packet he holds in his hands. 'No more chocolate, you see. Wasn't Ben looking into growing some?'

Mike frowns. 'He says it's too cold. Maybe in the future if it really does get warmer, but he says don't hold your breath.'

'That's a pity. I do miss the chocolate ones. And

sugar? Where are we on sugar?'

'Stan's due back any day now. He's bringing a load over the Remutaka Hill on horseback.'

'The cabbage trees aren't ready for harvesting yet?'

'No Derek, that's a long way off still. Years before we'll get any sugar that way. If at all.'

'And how about sailing to the Pacific to get it direct from the growers? Cut out the middleman. That was a thought, wasn't it?'

Derek smiles at Anton as if Mike's about to perform a difficult circus trick and Derek's saying 'watch this!'

Mike stares at Derek for a long time before taking a deep breath.

'No Derek. No one wants to sail, especially not all that way when you can get some from any dairy up north.'

Derek nods and sighs, then seems surprised to see Anton still standing there. 'Anyway, off you go. You and your birds. Do they need crumbs? Doris deals with the broken biscuits, I think.'

'Marge uses them for the slices, Derek,' says Mike.

'Oh yes, the slices. Only a woman over a certain age knows how to make a good slice. Have you tried one of her slices Anton?'

'I haven't had the pleasure, no.'

'You should. You really should. Cheerio then.'

Derek Hope waves the packet of gingernuts and turns to talk to an elderly couple who've been waiting to chat.

*

The market's always been a feature of the valley, but it used to be full of arts and crafts no one especially wanted or needed but were sometimes bought as gifts from stalls that would never have survived commercial conditions. Many hobbyists put their tinkerings on display each week like the original form of social media where any purchases were the equivalent of *likes*. For many, sales didn't compensate for the price of materials or labour, but they did serve to bolster fragile egos. For others it was a chance to pass the same twenty dollar note around from stall to stall each week and have a good natter in the meantime. And every now and then an excellent stall took *more than its fair share*, much to the annoyance of everyone.

Since the earthquake there's been a glut of wonky

stalls run by young newcomers still learning to weave, to build, to sew, to grow, to carve, to craft, to pot, to paint. Those fresh off the stagecoach creating all sorts of nonsense no one buys, but gradually sinking down to desperately trying to create a surplus to trade, to survive. It's becoming increasingly clear that many are there only until their resources from their parents run out and they move on. Hopefully move on. Else they stay and scrounge and generally make a nuisance of themselves.

The faces seem to continually change, people come, learn, or fail to learn, grow tired or disillusioned and leave and are replaced by others with again seemingly endless energy and enthusiasm. Some blend in so seamlessly that it's soon forgotten that they've not grown up here. But most stalls are still run by locals, and some locals have sat behind the same trestle table for years, or decades even.

Take Richard Byrd, for example, Dicky to his friends. He's lived in the valley for close to forty years but still has a strong Yorkshire accent. Luckily for him people used to watch *Emmerdale Farm* or read those vet books by Herriot. Wonderful books those. Can you imagine if he had been from Cornwall, or Newcastle?

No one would ever have understood a word!

Richard will have a yarn with anyone. Enjoys it. He's run the same second-hand book stall for twenty-eight of those years. Not the same stock anymore, of course, but a table at the market is still a pretty good bet for meeting people, getting out of the house, having a bit of a chin wag.

Back when it was still an arts and crafts market full of bits and bobs, the same second-hand junk going from stall to home to another stall to another home, Tim talked to him once. He found an old birding book on one of Dicky's tables, one of the many books with a name like: *A Field Guide to the Birds of New Zealand*, or *A Field Guide to New Zealand Birds*, or *New Zealand Birds: a Field Guide*. Tim, without knowing it, sounded like what Dicky would call *a bit of a swot* when he started referring to the books by their authors rather than the titles. The book Tim found at this market was the field guide by Falla, Sibson, and Turbott, one he hadn't seen before.

'For sale? For sale? For sale?'

Why would anybody sell such a beautiful book? It had, according to its cover, over two hundred illustrations. It included colour plates with the facing pages featuring numbered lists of birds. Tim stared at one of the pages for ages: *Rockhopper Penguin, Snares Crested Penguin, Erect-Crested Penguin, Gentoo Penguin.*

'That's why it's on the table, lad.' Richard grinned, hands in pockets, rocking back and forth on his heels watching Tim like he was a cockatiel in a cage.

Tim slowly turned the pages, keeping them closer to his face than seemed normal. 'How much how? Much?' he whispered.

These days it's different, of course, but Tim's question put Dicky in somewhat of a dilemma. He usually charged upwards of five dollars for a paperback; twenty and up for non-fiction. Normally a book like the field guide would have a faint pencil mark of thirty dollars at least on the inside cover. No doubt this would be why some books had been gracing Richard's table for decades, but Richard didn't mind. Her indoors, the long-suffering Annette, would just shake her head at the kitchen sink at the thought but Richard was happy enough with the arrangement. And that book had cost him a pretty penny, back in the day.

But here was this young lad, keen as mustard on an old man's sport. The way Tim cradled the book, gently stroking the pages and poring over the colour plates, he didn't look like one of these hooligans, one of those, those, those young things who would more than likely just set fire to the book as soon as look at it!

A good, firm price made people pay respect. Couldn't just give it away. And yet here was this young man …

Yes. It was a dilemma.

'Keen on birding, are you?'

Tim blinked. 'Birds I like, I like birds.'

'How much do *you* think it's worth?' Richard said. Taunted even. Never shy to have a laugh at someone else's expense. It's character building. He likes to help others build character.

Tim had stood still, Richard watching him like a kārearea waiting for a pigeon to fall into the precise line of sight needed to attack. Finally, Tim seemed to make up his mind and started searching through his pockets.

There was a bus ticket … for this was from the time when there were still buses; a matted tissue; a piece of beach glass from Point Howard; a mini compass; a blue ballpoint pen; a short pencil from the local pub given to kids for the puzzles on the placemats; a fluffy ball that could once have been a Fisherman's Friend cough lolly; a pocket knife with the toothpick missing; Crowe's *Pocket Guide to New Zealand Birds*; a mini notebook with a keyring but no keys; a metal nail file; an assortment of screws, nuts, bolts, nails, and washers; a letter in an envelope where the edges were so worn away the layers of paper looked like layers of sediment in a geological fault; a keyring with a solitary key; and three dollars sixty in change.

Tim picked the pocket fluff off the coins and held his palm up and out towards Derek like an offering of bread to a tame duck.

'Ahh, well now. That book's worth more than a few coins, you know.'

'Three, three, the dollars sixty.'

'Three dollars sixty, you say! That, my lad, would only buy you one chapter in a grand book like this.'

'One chapter? One?'

Now, that was the moment when Dicky should have noticed a change in Tim's voice, a slight lifting of the vowels, of the eyebrows, of the hopes. But Richard was not really a salesman. That book could have stayed forgotten on the table for another thirty years and he wouldn't really have minded, while if he sold it for less than it was worth he would have regretted it for the rest of his life. All he heard was Tim sigh.

Tim flipped to the index: Kiwi; Penguins; Grebes; Albatrosses; Petrels, Shearwaters and Fulmars; Storm Petrels; Diving Petrels; Tropic Birds; Gannets and Boobies; Shags or Cormorants; Frigate Birds; Herons, Egrets and Bitterns; Ibises and Spoonbills; Geese, Swans and Ducks; Harrier-Hawks and Eagles; Falcons; Game Birds; Rails, Crakes, Weka, Gallinules and Coots; Waders, Oystercatchers; Plovers and Dotterels; Curlews, Godwits, Snipe and Sandpipers; Stilts and Avocets; Phalaropes; Pratincoles; Skuas; Gulls, Terns and Noddies; Pigeons and Doves; Parrots and Parakeets; Cuckoos; Owls; Swifts; Kingfishers; Rollers; New Zealand Wrens; Larks; Swallows and Martins; Cuckoo-Shrikes; Bulbuls; Flycatchers; Warblers; Thrushes; Accentors; Pipits and Wagtails; Honeyeaters; Silvereyes; Finches and Buntings; Sparrows and Weavers; Starlings; Crows; Australian Bell Magpies; New Zealand Wattle-Birds; New Zealand Thrushes.

He was heading for the page on Godwits when he passed *Plate 17: Some birds of Garden, Bush, and Scrub.* It included the Long-Tailed Cuckoo, Shining Cuckoo, Rifleman, Silvereye, Brown Creeper, Grey Warbler,

Whitehead, Rock Wren, Bush Wren, and Yellowhead. Not a terribly exciting list for most of us perhaps, but for Tim it was like looking at a photo of long-lost friends, a family photo. A family photo was something that Tim did not have in his pockets.

So, although not strictly a chapter, Tim closed the colour plate page and the facing page containing the list of names and neatly, swiftly, ripped them out of the book. He placed the three dollars sixty on the table and said, 'Thank you, thanking you.'

That's one thing you can always say about that Timothy, he does have good manners.

*

'Hold up a sec,' Mike calls out to Anton as he stops at the target range. Despite a recent effort to allow only *wholesome* stalls, the fairground type stands are still appearing from nowhere, popping up like mushrooms after the rain. On the far wall there are targets of varying sizes with words scrawled across each one in blue vivid: rimu bowl; pine chopping-board; jar of jam; jar of cauliflower and zucchini relish; one hour of light gardening work; one cubic metre of firewood (gum); matching fake fur cushions; large kete; candy floss.

Mike picks up an air rifle and checks the sights.

'What's the damage?' he says.

The guy behind the counter doesn't look up from what looks like a remarkably old newspaper.

'Three shots for a piece of fruit, two veggies, or a tradeable promissory note for work.'

'I have dried meat or fish.'

The paper goes down and the man stands up, looking around furtively. He leans in close.

'Keep your voice down. We're not supposed to accept any animal products. It's the new edict.'

'Since when?'

'Since this morning.'

'Ah, for fuck's sake. So, you don't want any then?'

'Don't be a dick, of course I do,' he says in a low voice. 'Give me some meat and take as many shots as you want.'

Mike pulls a small package wrapped in *Woman's Weekly* pages out of his backpack. He casually places it on the table and the man drops his newspaper over the top before slipping it out of sight under the trestle table.

'I only need one,' says Mike.

He tucks the butt of the rifle into his shoulder and lightly rests his finger on the trigger. Meat is, of course, far too much to pay, but keeping on the good side of a guy who has access to guns and ammo, and who travels in and out of the valley is a smart thing to do, even if these are only air rifles. And there's two ways to get on side with such a bloke – supply him in meat or show him you're a good shot.

Mike can do both.

The gun pops like the sound of a duck bobbing underwater and one of the paper targets shows a perfect bullseye.

The man says nothing but gives a little nod while closing his eyes briefly – a sign of profound respect. He lifts the prize, a bag of candy floss, out of a blue bin under the table. Insubstantial, innutritious, in a plastic bag, but highly sought after by some, a symbol of a lost world, a quick hit of nostalgia. It would have to have been carried in, of course, brought down from the north. Some would say a waste of time and effort to transport something so unnecessary. The respect Mike's earned from the meat and the marksmanship has been lessened somewhat by the choice of prize he aimed at. Mike can tell by the look in the fella's eyes. But it's a good shot, that can't be denied.

Mike nods at the targets and speaks to Anton.

'Want to try your luck.'

'Me? No! Oh no, no thank you.'

The man behind the counter rolls his eyes in solidarity with Mike and turns to replace the paper target. Mike picks up the bag of spun sugar and strolls through the market.

There are similar looking stalls selling similar looking goods staffed by similar looking people. There's some contraband, of course, like canned foods and mink blankets and tarpaulins and other imported products banned by the Community Board. But none of the stuff Mike really needs or wants. No ammunition, no hunting knives, no plastic bags, no boots, no warm clothing that isn't brightly coloured handknitted shawls or cardigans. Darren built a forge to make local knives until the valley declared itself carbon neutral and banned his stall.

They walk around the corner and find Tim rifling through old books.

'Got some crappy half-rate prize at the target practice,' says Mike. 'Just looking for a bin to put it in.

Have you seen one?'

Tim's eyes widen. Anton is fixated by Tim's hands, which have been flying around his body like flies on a corpse, but now settle into squirming grub-like fingers crawling around and around each other in a ball.

'Unless … you … you don't want it, do you?'

Mike holds up the bag briefly between thumb and forefinger like a piece of roadkill, then lobs it at Tim, and turns away. Tim fumbles for the bag, drops it, picks it up, hugs it close.

'I like it, yes, I like it, I like it very much.'

'Yeah, whatever. It'll rot your teeth. Come on Anton, we need to get you sorted.'

They walk past more stalls as Tim lags further and further behind until he finally sits down in the gutter and eats the candy floss by the handful.

'He'll be as sick as a dog later,' says Mike, as they wait some way off.

Anton watches Tim.

'I don't get it,' he says.

'Get what?'

'I assume you're a good shot, yes?'

Mike screws up his face and moves his chin out in a way that communicates, 'Of course.'

'So, you could've shot any of those targets … but you chose the candy floss.'

Mike pulls out some tobacco and starts rolling a smoke.

'Of course.' He licks the paper and rolls but doesn't light up. 'But Tim can't.' He points at the sticky, happy mess with his unlit smoke. 'He can't shoot for shit.'

Anton searches Mike's face, looking for something more. But there's nothing.

Mike cups his hand and lights up giving Tim enough time to catch up, grinning, sugar stuck to his face, in his hair, on his hands. Mike shakes his head.

'Come on you useless bastards, get a move on. I've got better stuff to do than babysit you two losers.' He focuses on Anton. 'What are you going to do about food? There's no supermarket here, you know. If you need food, you need to get it now, market day's only once a week.'

'That's fine, I have funds, a grant came through you see.'

'Cash is no good. Save it for any stuff you need to bring in later. You need skills to trade, items to sell. You don't have a veggie garden up and running yet, though it's not too late to put one in. You can't hunt or fish, you said, so that's out. Can you dig?'

'Dig?'

Mike looks Anton up and down. 'No, you've never done any manual labour in your life, have you? Pity. They're putting in new sewer lines to drain the shit away from the main housing and it's decent work if you can get it. The olds have a monopoly on baking and preserving, so that's no good. Tell me, what *can* you do?'

Anton thinks of all the skills he has. He can create rather elaborate databases, format spreadsheets, do a stunning amount of boring data entry for hours on end without complaint or error, find information in old non-digitised peer-reviewed periodicals that no one else can be bothered tracking down, check colleagues' reference lists for punctuation typos, write lectures for others, write articulately, even amusingly. He's written a couple of conference speeches but hasn't been able to summon enough courage to present them to an audience (he gave that task to a fellow student who shared authoring rights but none of the research or writing load). But standing in the middle of the valley, right now, he can't think of any skills that anyone would want.

When Anton remains silent, Mike sighs.

'I figured. Right, you owe me.'

He reaches into his backpack and pulls out some more packages wrapped in *Woman's Weekly*, puts them into Anton's arms and places a few potatoes and wrinkled beetroot on top.

'Go get yourself some seedlings and seeds. You can borrow our tools.'

'I don't know what to buy.'

'Tell Bill you're with me and need a starter kit. Say you've got Mike's food to pay for them but don't let anyone else see what you've got. He'll see you right.'

Anton watches Mike turn and walk off through the crowd. The children run around the grown-ups, screaming, laughing, playing tag. Anton carries his soil covered *money* along the path until he sees a table covered in gardening tools and trays of seedlings. An elderly man with a wispy white comb-over greets him warmly.

'Let me guess,' says Bill, 'The university man, here to get his starter pack?'

'How did you know?'

'You're kidding right? You're the Bird Man! We all know all about you, my son.'

Mike and Anton walk away from the market, across boardwalks made from old packing cases resting on top of the liquefaction. The houses they pass are mostly boarded up or have fallen down. The two young men walk slightly uphill towards the edge of the suburb where houses skirt the native bush.

'Mike?'

Mike raises his eyebrows in a way that Anton takes to mean he can continue talking.

'Um. So, it seems like everyone I meet already knows who I am.'

'Yup.'

Anton waits for more, but nothing comes.

'I wasn't expecting that. I was, well, I was planning to come and collect my data, and—'

'Look, everyone has to contribute. You want to go and sit in the bush and listen to your birds? Yeah, well, don't we all, mate. Don't we all. But where are you going to get your food from? You expect someone else to grow and harvest the food and cook for you? And for what?'

Anton stops walking. He stands there with his arms full of supplies from the market, supplies he's bought with Mike's *money*. He feels sheepish.

'Well, I do want you to know I appreciate—'

'Look, everyone knows who you are because first of all we need to know you're not going to be a sponger. We've had so many people come in, thinking they're going to live off-grid but still wanting their soy lattes that we just need to know you're legit. Then Derek has plans to make all this into a bird sanctuary. Not a bad idea in itself, good old-fashioned conservation that will actually protect the birds. But it's all tied up with bureaucracy and infighting with the Tourism Committee who want more people, the Eco Squad who want fewer people, and the local government who want to get rid of everybody so they can give it all over to shady developers to rebuild. Then there's those who don't like outsiders coming in, full stop, not helped by all the idealists wanting to create some sort of utopia but unwilling or unable to help build it. Derek reckons with your credentials and research then they just might get funding for the sanctuary.'

'My research isn't really designed to do that, I

would rather just be left alone, to be honest, and—'

'Doesn't matter what you want. There are a whole bunch of factions here who think you and your research can help or hinder them in their ambitions. And passions can run pretty hot when you're discussing people's homes and livelihoods. So, you're going to have to figure out whose side you're on.'

'I would really rather not take sides.'

'You won't survive here alone. No one can go it alone. So perhaps think about it this way. Whose help do you need the most to achieve what *you* want? Figure that out and then you'll know whose side you're on.'

'And you?' says Anton. 'Whose side are you on?'

'Some of us are just trying to keep our heads above water.'

Mike takes a turn and starts walking up a slope, up a road that rises above the liquefaction. A road lined with houses that look largely unscathed or at least professionally patched up.

'This here is Kōwhai Grove,' Mike calls back over his shoulder as Anton rushes to catch up.

A kererū dislodges itself from a kowhai tree up the hill, swoops down to what was once a telephone line and sits bobbing between Mike and Anton, albeit up high.

'Most of the houses have the original owners. They're a tough breed up here. Refused to be evacuated. And, being homeowners, the government can't evict them as easily as they could with all us renters. Most of them are elderly and own their places outright so they don't need to take many lodgers, except the likes of Marie who you're staying with because she likes the company. That corner house is Derek's, the so-called mayor. And that's Henry Masters, he's 2IC, there. Thinks he's in charge of the whole street.'

Mike waves at a man in his late sixties who scowls before giving a begrudging nod.

'He hasn't shaken hands with anyone since the lurgy, but was never too friendly to begin with, so don't be offended. Next door's Susan Harris.'

Anton sees the venetian blinds snap shut.

'And then there's Mr Henderson.'

An elderly man stands at his lounge window sipping hot tea. He raises the mug in greeting.

'He's alright. He'll break your hand if he shakes it, but he'll probably be wary for a few weeks. Give him time. And opposite him is Mrs Henderson.'

A small grey-haired woman is filling a birdbath from a watering can. She smiles and gives a little wave.

They get to the end of the cul-de-sac where a long white house overlooks the whole street.

'And here's Marie.' Mike grins. 'You're going to love Marie; she just loves to chat.'

Anton can't be sure, but Mike appears to enjoy watching Anton flinch.

*

It's almost as though no one any longer knows what Mr and Mrs Henderson's names are, including Mr and Mrs Henderson. Mr Henderson lives at number six Kōwhai Grove. Mrs Henderson lives at number three, in a white house with blue shutters, the ones that are screwed to the walls so serve no practical purpose whatsoever and are too narrow to cover the windows even if someone ever thought to attach them with hinges. But there was a time when, if you had a little extra money, you put shutters on the windows, cast-concrete bird-tables on the lawn, gnomes under the hedge, butterflies with immovable wings on the outer walls.

Mr Henderson's number six happens, by a quirk of section sizes along the street, to be directly opposite number three. Number three's the original marital home and being so is more comfortable thanks to insulation, heating, a ramp to the front door with a handrail to replace the original three steps, and an established garden. Being the marital home it's full of memories no doubt and many have said, over the years, that Mrs Henderson should sell, start over, but such a thing has seemingly never occurred to her.

Their houses are mirror images of one another. It's not as unusual in Awaawa as you might think. In the 1960s there were three main developers, who only used three to four plans each. It was cheaper that way. You could have one crew only ever make one plan, that way the houses were quicker to build, cheaper to build, more profitable to sell. So, to make the streets look more interesting, more attractive to home buyers, the plans were rotated 90 degrees, 180 degrees, flipped and rotated again. The unlucky had the lounge facing south and the laundry, toilet, bathroom, and kitchen getting all day sun. Mr and Mrs Henderson both live in a Kevin Carpenter Homes Plan Number Four, flipped on the lounge and front door side so that Mr

Henderson's house reflects Mrs Henderson's across the street, looking just like the reflection in the goldfish pond he once built with his son in the front garden. Mrs Henderson tried to keep the pond stocked with lovely little fish but the kingfishers, the cats, even that daft dog they had for years used to pick the fish out, one by one, until they were all gone. Mr Henderson eventually filled it in and planted begonias.

The old neighbours know the daily habits and any newcomers, if they're observant enough, learn them quickly too. Each morning Mr and Mrs Henderson pull open their dining room curtains at seven a.m. They stare into each other's eyes lovingly for a moment, or so the romantics in the street like to believe, or else they glare at each other in a battle that has raged on for years, as the children and the divorced in the street like to imagine. The truly observant, as opposed to the merely nosy, might sometimes see a flutter of a wave from Mrs Henderson, followed by the faintest of nods from Mr Henderson. If you mention this though, it will probably be dismissed as Parkinson's.

After curtains are opened the odd couple busy themselves with the making of porridge and cups of tea. Mr Henderson likes to sneak a spoonful of raspberry jam into the bottom of the bowl, while Mrs Henderson drizzles rewarewa honey from an old milk jug. Sometimes, if he's lucky, Mr Henderson pours a moat of cream into the bowl after adding just a splash to his tea. He does the crossword, if Tim has managed to find him any on his travels, while Mrs Henderson reads the gossip columns, no matter how outdated, and looks for any celebrity weddings she's missed to cut out for her scrapbook.

Tim was the one who noticed that it was jars of jam or lemon honey that Mrs Henderson dropped in the letterbox of number six and not bags of dog turds as Henry had said. Tim also thought that when Mr Henderson cut the hedges at number three when Mrs Henderson went to play bridge on Wednesdays, he did not appear to be harbouring fantasies of snipping Mrs Henderson into long slender slices, as was Susan's opinion. But when Tim tells anyone these observations they're dismissed.

That guy Henderson, he beat her, the nasty man; Mrs Henderson cheated on him with the last minister who had to leave in disgrace, and she could never show her face in church again; the dog slept on the bed and she said, 'It's me or the dog!'; Mrs Henderson adopted every stray cat around and the house stank of cat piss; they had a child who died and they never forgave one another (she drowned the baby in the bathtub because he wouldn't stop screaming; he smacked their teenage daughter over the head with a shovel when she threatened to tell her mum he'd been touching her); he was mean as muck and wanted the higher single person's pension but Mrs Henderson, being painfully honest, never spoke to him again for fear that the government would drag him off to jail for benefit fraud.

Or something along those lines.

They remind Tim of bookends. A couple so alike, so in tune, so completely the epitome of what *the other half* implies that they look alike, act alike, dress alike. They finish each other's sentences, wear similar clothes, look more like siblings than spouses or former husband and wife or whatever it is that they now are. She's still Mrs Henderson after all. She hasn't changed her name. You can imagine they are the type to settle into the washing and drying of dishes with no apparent communication as to whose turn it is. They're the kind of couple that never spends a day apart and call each other Mum and Dad long after the kids have left home, and eventually die within hours of one another.

'And that was the problem with those two,' says Marie to Anton and she pours his tea. All he'd done was mention he'd seen signs of both Mr and Mrs Henderson as he walked up Kōwhai Grove. He's been sitting at the kitchen table for three hours drinking endless cups of tea and has not even seen his room yet. He feels like he knows everyone already, whether he wants to or not, as Marie shares so much detail on all the inhabitants of the street. Despite himself he can't help but be curious about the Hendersons.

'Is that why they split up, they were too similar? They got on each other's nerves?'

'No, no,' says Marie as she draws on a fag. 'Why? Is that what your parents are like?'

'No!' Anton shifts in his seat uncomfortably.

Marie lifts her eyebrows meaningfully, but Anton doesn't speak eyebrow fluently and doesn't know to oblige her with details. Instead, he asks another question.

'Were they sick of each other? Time to move on?'

Marie sighs, shakes her head, and continues.

'They had a son, Carl. Nice boy. Did well at school and went off to London, he did. It's alright for some, I suppose.' She taps the cigarette on the edge of a lacquered pāua shell ashtray Mr Henderson made years ago. 'Did well for himself, though I don't remember him ever sending back any money for his parents to visit. That's what he should've done, of course, them supporting him through uni, and all. Not cheap, that sort of education. You'd know all about that, I suppose.' She points her cigarette at Anton. 'And he must have had loads of dough, working in London like he was. I've never been there, of course, my parents brought me straight here. London's a nice place to live, is it?'

'I wouldn't know, I'm from a bit further north.'

Marie takes another long drag and looks up at the fly-spotted ceiling and squints as though there's writing up there that she's trying to decipher. 'Was there quite a few years I seem to remember. But he would have been about your age I'm guessing ...'

Marie cocks her head to the side and appraises Anton's features. Anton, not used to being scrutinised, feels his face redden.

'So, they were sad?' he says. 'Sad that he'd gone

overseas? And they split up?'

'No dear, I don't think so. Well, yes, they were sad, but not overly so. She got the second bedroom back and turned it into a sewing room, well a craft room really. Arnold wanted it for a woodwork room, but he already had the garage and sleepout, so it was only fair that she have it. No, young Carl was killed in a car crash in Europe somewhere. Greece? Italy? Somewhere with olives I seem to remember, though goodness knows why I'd remember that, of all things. Nasty tasting little things. They had to have him cremated which was a crying shame. It's very expensive to bring the body back, isn't it? You know how it is.'

Anton doesn't know how it is but nods anyway. 'And the grief caused them to separate?'

'No! God love you, you're an odd one, aren't you?' She taps the cigarette again and squints at him. 'Are you sure your parents aren't divorced?'

Anton shakes his head.

'No? Oh well, of course they grieved, even fought a little, but don't you say I said that!' She waggles her finger. 'It's only normal to have the odd tiff when you lose a child. Be strange not to. No, no, they just couldn't get out of the habit of calling each other Mum and Dad.'

'Oh …'

'I was there one time, having a nice cuppa, not long after he passed. I was at the kitchen table with Evelyn when Arnold came in all excited, with a great big zucchini, well, marrow I suppose. Huge it was. And Arnold said, *Look at the size of this one, Mum!* Well, I didn't know which way to look, thinking he was being a bit, you know, rude.'

Marie nods at Anton's crotch and raises her eyebrows. Anton gulps and crosses his legs.

'Well, I didn't know which way to look, but then Evelyn, God love her, tried to change the subject, and said, *Would you like a cuppa tea, Dad?* Well, that was it. A big fat tear rolled down Arnold's face and then Evelyn started weeping and grabbed her hanky from her bosom and tried to hide her face, all the while nattering on about her powder. Neither of them is big on crying in public, not even at the memorial service they had. So, I made my leave and left them to it. Wasn't long after that Arnold moved across to Aaron Little's house. Sad story that one, Aaron lost his wife to cancer, don't you know? Then he died of a broken heart only three months later. It's often the way.'

The conversation turns to the late Mrs Aaron Little, as Marie refers to her, but Anton's still thinking about the Hendersons.

Eventually Marie shows Anton his room. It's neat and tidy, clean, but circa late eighties or thereabouts. Shiny white wallpaper with pink and lilac flowers, dusky pink carpet, a bedside cabinet with homemade doilies on top and a ceramic and brass lamp, and a crisp white bedspread on a single bed.

'No women!' is all she says as she leaves the room and quietly closes the door.

Anton looks out his window and can see every house all the way down the street. The sun reaches the horizon over the peak of the hill and Anton watches as the curtains at number three and number six are pulled at the same time in the dining rooms, the ones for the ranch sliders that lead out onto matching patios. The last curtains to be pulled are for the bedrooms facing each other. Mrs and Mrs Henderson stand for a moment staring at each other. Mr Henderson rests his fingers gently on the glass and Mrs Henderson places one hand on the window and another on her chest and closes her eyes. The last rays of sunlight show every speck of dust hovering in the air of the dining room at number six and make Anton think of a snow globe.

*

It's morning and Anton's surprised to see Mike and Tim at the kitchen table tucking into bacon and eggs.

'There you are!' says Marie. 'Thought you were going to miss out.' She takes a plate piled high with food out of the oven and pops it on a placemat at the table.

'Oh. I thought there's no electricity here?'

'There's not. I've got bottled gas. Gavin, that's my late husband, insisted on gas. He was from the old country and didn't like faffing about waiting for a pan to heat up. Drove him mad, it did. Didn't it, Mike?'

'Aye, Marie. It did.' He turns his head slightly towards Anton, 'The houses on hillsides always had bottled gas. No mains up here.' He resumes shovelling food into his mouth like he hasn't eaten in a week.

Anton thinks it might not be so bad here after all. 'A cooked breakfast every morning sounds like heaven.'

Mike lifts a cup, ignoring the handle put there for that purpose, and takes a long drink while eyeing

Anton over the rim. 'Every morning? You'd be lucky.'

Marie, her head tilted to the side, appraises Anton. 'You are an odd one, aren't you love? It's a special occasion.'

'What's the occasion?' says Anton.

'Well, you're here of course, you dilly! And you'll need a good breakfast in you to get through what we've planned for today.'

'Planned for today? I was rather thinking I could get into the bush, have a scout around?'

Marie chuckles. 'Well, it was supposed to be a surprise, but,' she glances around as though checking no one else is in the room before putting up a hand and saying in a stage whisper, 'The thing is, we've got a bit of a welcome party for you.' She raises her eyebrows, and bites her bottom lip, watching intently for Anton's reaction.

'Oh. Um. Well, that's awfully nice of you, but I'm not really a party person.'

'That's good,' says Mike gruffly as he stands and takes his plate to the sink. 'Because it's not really a party, eh?'

'It's more of a carnival,' says Marie.

'A carnival?' says Anton frowning.

'A carnival, a festival, a fistful of carnival!' says Tim laughing, spraying food out of his mouth.

Mike leans against the sink, breaks a matchstick in half and starts using it to clean between his teeth.

'The local Community Board thought of a *genius* way to help you with your little project. The whole street's involved and a fair few others too.'

Mike looks at the matchstick as he talks. He doesn't seem very enthusiastic. He resumes picking his teeth as he watches Anton.

Anton gulps.

'Well, that's awfully kind. Very thoughtful, but I'm, well —'

'Wouldn't do for you to miss your own welcome party, now, would it?' says Mike. 'Not seeing as everyone has been working so hard on the preparations?'

Anton swallows hard.

'No, right. No, it wouldn't. I'd, um, love to come.'

Marie beams and claps her hands.

'I'll get the things.'

'Good lad,' says Mike slapping Anton hard on the back as he walks past.

Tim remains at the table, grinning, egg yolk on his

chin.

*

Andira Chakor holds her red and orange sari in her hands. Seven metres of silk hangs in loops, the same hue as the bricks of the houses that used to line the valley floor and now form the brick path leading to her front door. Her husband Garunda carted the bricks up wheelbarrow after wheelbarrow after wheelbarrow. It's as though an enormous chip of baked clay flaked off in the earthquake, flaked off so thinly that it flew up into her hands and she holds it flapping in the wind. Red earth covered in semi-precious jewels and embroidered flowers.

Some might say it's far too special a sari for an occasion such as this, but it's nice, isn't it, to get out and celebrate for a change? Some remember when the teenagers in the Chakor family threw pork sausages over the fence dividing their semi-detached house from the Shahbaz family's during Ramadan, and the Shahbaz teenagers threw beef sausages over the fence during Diwali. Andira and Zara were appalled and would pause at the fence and apologise, swap, and debate the merits of various punishments, interventions, and enticements to make them stop, while the younger children played tag, jumping the fence or raced their bikes around the back. It was only after the Hope children from number one, Jemima, Jonah, and Jayson, had hurled eggs at all the houses in the street one Halloween, that the meat wars had ended. And who, in their right minds, could have foreseen that? The act was so shockingly American it united the entire street, including the teens, against such things and all aerial assaults immediately ceased.

It's generally agreed that it's important to look good on public occasions such as this one. Zara has long reams of cloth that the whole family holds up between them. Perhaps longer even than the seven metres held by Andira as she waited for the children and grandchildren to come join her. Perhaps Andira was miffed at the excess in length displayed by Zara, but Komas used to own the fabric shop between the Abra-kebab-bra and Pasifika Palace. Zara therefore owned a lot of cloth so it's hardly fair to compare.

Mrs Henderson wasn't at all sure about the Shahbaz family when they first arrived as young newlyweds, but they had a son born around the same time, so she and Zara swapped stories over the fence while the two boys poked sticks into each other's eyes, went to school together, fought over the same girls, raced cars along the stretch of road to the north. Zak Shahbaz stayed in the valley and took over the day to day running of the fabric shop after Komas' stroke, and the family has always done a rather a good line in net curtains of which Mrs Henderson's especially fond. She's taken down the bone white curtains in the spare bedroom and they glare in the morning sun.

Across the road Mr Henderson clutches his best crocheted blanket. It's a proper one made with short pieces of leftover wool from other projects, and therefore contains colours that clash violently with one another. It's not one of those acrylic numbers made with machines overseas that they used to sell over at the mall. Oh no. This one was made by Mrs Henderson, when her husband's knees had first started giving him gyp. (There, right there's another piece of evidence for the doubters that they still love one another. Although, admittedly, one could also say that by bringing it out for the festival, of all days, he doesn't care if it gets torn or unravelled. But then again, if it needs darning then it will give him another excuse to pop over and have a chat with the missus … ahhh, every new piece of evidence as to the state of their marriage births at least three new theories.)

Ryan and Jessica, the relatively new and young homeowners on the street who bought just before the land rose and the prices fell, each grip matching lavalava they brought back from their honeymoon in Samoa. The purchase seemed so right at the time in the bleaching sunlight of the equator, but at home the colours are, admittedly, somewhat garish. Not even suitable for a jaunt up Grawler track over to Day's Bay. But surely, they're just the thing for the festival? Not a wasted purchase after all! What a relief to find a use for them. Jessica completes the scene with the inclusion of a flower in her hair.

The Ioane children opposite always seem to be laughing. Ahh, such happy children. But why were they pointing at Ryan and Jessica? What could possibly be so funny? Sia and Fitu shush them. Andrew, Peter, and Josephine stop laughing and stand still and serene, holding long lengths of tapa cloth between them. Their cousins line up beside them along the fence line. And not two but three grandmothers are propped up between visiting aunts and uncles from other parts of the valley.

Fitu passes a bowl of panikeke across to Henry who by now knows the drill and passes a plate of pikelets back. Mrs Henderson pops over the road to pass a jar of strawberry jam to add some sweetness, which is much appreciated now that banana and pineapple are so hard to come by.

It's 9 a.m. and by now most people are at their front gates. There's talk of weather and children and which vegetables are coming up nicely thank you very much. Even Tim's here. Marie has Anton holding the other end of a crocheted mat made with old plastic bags, rags, threadbare clothes, and bits and pieces, added to most recently just the night before. Now, it's longer than the space it recently occupied from one end of the hall to the other and one end will have to be rolled up in future. It's colour coordinated, mostly blues and greens washing into whites, yellows, and greys. It looks like the sea is lapping at the gate.

Anton looks uncomfortable. Lost even. It's unknown, as yet, whether this is the way he normally wears his face or if he's just still settling in.

It's a funny party, thinks Anton. Everybody's standing outside their own doors or gates and not really congregating. People seem cheerful, friendly, but they wave across the road at each other, or call out down the street, instead of walking up to one another. Everybody, it seems, is holding some sort of fabric. Mostly exceedingly long pieces of cloth held between two or more people. But there's also individuals holding tea towels, tablecloths, sarongs, scarves, flags, fabric remnants.

Ava comes out of the flat with Phoebe, Tui, and Jay.

'Got your kete?' calls Henry over the fences.

Tui rolls her eyes. Ava shows no emotion, no sign of having heard, but slowly, carefully unfurls a Bob Marley blanket which she and Tui hold over their heads. Phoebe holds up her latest flax mat, her arms sore from all the scouring of the flax, but she smiles broadly. Jay chats to Henry by the fence about the best methods for preserving lemons.

It suddenly becomes quiet.

'Shh,' says Tim.

'Shh,' says Marie to Anton even though he's not talking. 'It's almost time.'

A solitary moggy, grey with white stripes, walks to the centre of the road and sits down. She starts to clean her back leg in slow careful strokes. Everyone's watching her. No one speaks.

She reaches her toes. She spreads them wide and alternates biting them and licking between them. Bob and Doris, from over Mr Henderson's back fence, have their grandson Daniel down the valley for the day and he grips, but can't wave, an oversized Rugby World Cup flag. It's surely older than he is. Daniel doesn't wonder about the age of the flag; he wonders why the cat doesn't giggle. He always giggles when his father dries between his toes after a bath.

The cat seems unaware of her audience. How could she not notice a street full of people watching her?

The people wait.

The grey and white moggy is joined by another cat. This one's the colour of Ryan's once trendy beard. His ears seem unusually large for a cat, emphasised by the fact he starts cleaning one of them first. He licks his paw, flattens the ear forwards, it springs back, and he licks his paw again. You know you shouldn't stare but really, have you ever seen such large ears on a cat before? And so orange!

And all at once there's more. Fluffy cats with

attitude and short haired ones with skinny limbs. Fat ones with dilated pupils and scrawny diseased ones with gunk in their eyes and weeping wounds. Purebreds and white ones with sunburnt ears. There's that lame one who always steals the milk that Mrs Henderson leaves out for the hedgehogs and the cat with a white tail like a duster that Defor, being a greyhound, likes to chase. Marie's blue tinged cat that can't, some say won't, jump or climb trees, waddles to join the others.

The magnolia in the Ioane garden's littered with budding kittens and the hedges between Marie's and Susan's gardens contain claws like thorns, and meows that can't be seen.

It's time to begin.

Saris and net curtains and blankets and tapa and tea towels and lavalava and flags are waved and flapped. Rugs are shaken and dressing gowns shiver with excitement. The kids run down the road, arms above their heads holding sheets that fly like capes behind them. They run between the legs of adults and the cats run between the legs of the children.

The cats and the kids compete for screeching effectiveness. The toddlers have the volume, the children the pitch, but the cats have the confidence of those who know they can't be caught, can't be threatened with bed and no dessert.

Susan puts in her earplugs.

The sound of silks snapping in the breeze is unlike that of the snap of a tea towel against the naked skins of one's calves. Quilts have a quality that quietens the air. Saris send the sounds singing. Flags create a guttural sound that causes young men, without even noticing, to walk in a rhythm not unlike a march.

It takes hours.

Cats are chased up trees and across roofs and through hedges. They're chased in all directions and net curtains are knotted up with blankets, and saris and hijabs become entangled and the holes in the blankets get bigger where the cats have broken through. Lavalava lingers on lampposts before being whipped off in the wind to sail down the street with children chasing along behind.

They don't catch a single cat.

The residents finally stop, hands clutching fenceposts, fingers pressed against the stitch in their sides, or they stand in the centre of the road, hands on hips, chests heaving.

Children are scooped up and taken home for naps. Casualties are counted, disinfectant applied, and plasters distributed.

The neighbours talk excitedly of the perfectly good curtains ruined, the missing sequins, the unfurling embroidery, frayed fabric, flax matting falling apart. They inspect the tiny punctures, the massive holes, the rips, the ragged seams.

Oh, but wasn't it fantastic! Invigorating! We *must* do this again. Next time we'll catch the cats. Yes indeed! Spontaneous get-togethers are arranged so neighbours can continue telling their tales. All the kids disappear down the street to the playground with their sheets and their scarves to re-enact the most exciting of scenes. The elderly venture inside for a cuppa and perhaps even a lie down. Men and women chat over the fences. Marie beams at Anton.

'Wasn't that just wonderful!'

Derek leans over the front gate and chimes in.

'Thrilling!'

'Did you see …?'

And they're off, recounting stitches lost, cat fur gained, blow by blow accounts of the whole event.

No one seems to notice Anton as they wander away

and he's left alone on the lawn holding the unravelling mat from the hall.

He's like a cat with the remnants of a ball of string.

The cats sit in trees and on windowsills cleaning their faces. They sit brazenly on lawns and in the centre of the road, atop cars and on fence posts. They're busy leaving fur on sofas and flattening the native grasses in the sunny spots in the gardens. They sit on kitchen tables and lounge on front steps.

An enormous ginger tom appears from the bushes and rubs his head against Anton's legs. Back and forth he goes, headbutting the back of Anton's knees making him feel unsteady on his feet, unsettled.

Finally, the cat curls into a ball at Anton's feet, closes his eyes, and begins to purr.

*

It's night and Anton's in a deep sleep. A hand reaches out of the dark to grab his shoulder and shake him awake.

'Oi, get up. Pack your sleeping gear and a change of warm clothes.'

Anton sits up and rubs his eyes.

'What time is it?'

'Come on,' Mike whispers. 'We're going on a trip.'

'A trip? I had rather hoped to get started on my data collection; I need —'

'You *need* to pack a bag.'

Mike climbs out the sash window and paces back and forth on the lawn smoking. He seems agitated. As he packs his bag Anton wonders if he's done something wrong. He looks at his notebooks, his birding books, his laptop, and thinks about taking them, but hesitates. He's spent the last few days helping Marie with *odd jobs* and being introduced around the neighbourhood having endless cups of tea. No one, it seems, wants him to start doing any research. He's surprised to realise that makes him feel somewhat relieved. He pops his head out the window.

'I'll need to tell Marie if I'm not going to be home for … breakfast? Lunch?'

'I've left her a note. Come on, we haven't got all day.'

Anton wants to point out it's the middle of the night, but he lets it pass. He often points out things like that and it doesn't make him popular so he's trying to curb the habit.

They walk down the path onto Kōwhai Grove and head not down but up the road to the bush track. It's still dark so Anton pulls out his torch.

'Put that away,' Mike hisses.

The torch goes away and so does Anton's breath. What's all this about? Is he being taken out of the valley? Has he failed some sort of test? Is he being evicted? But then why not bring all his belongings? Would they steal his laptop? Would they do away with him? He's heard some of the rumours about this place.

Stop it, Anton tells himself. Just stop it!

Once they're in the bush Mike hands Anton a torch that metes out the smallest amount of light needed to see his way, allowing him just enough to see the dark shadow of Mike in front of him. They trudge in silence up to the ridge track then north towards the hill road. When they reach the spot where they had first met, Mike sits down on the clay bank and takes out his tobacco. He doesn't offer Anton any, not that Anton would have accepted.

The rolly is lit, the first puff taken, and Mike uses it to point into the darkness, presumably in the direction of the city across the harbour.

'We're heading out. If you chunder, I'll throw you

overboard.'

'Out in the harbour?'

The day he came across the harbour it was what Marie would have described as *flat as piddle on the floor*. But he'd still been queasy. Now there's a strong northerly blowing and the water will be choppy, and he feels like spewing just thinking about it.

'I'm not really too good in boats, not, well I don't exactly have my sea legs. I'm not sure that I can be of that much assistance to you. If, well, assistance is what you're after.'

'I need an extra pair of hands. Someone who knows not to blab. Is that you?'

Anton nods, realises it's dark, and quickly says yes clearly and without any other comment. Sometimes he manages to not completely fuck things up for himself.

By the time they walk down the hill to the foreshore Anton's talked himself into it. Talked himself into not being sick or going green or looking like he won't be useful after all. He grabs the other side of the boat hidden in the bush, helps to slide it down and get it in the water without letting go. He grazes his knuckles but doesn't call out, even when the salty water sloshes over them.

Mike holds the boat as Anton clambers in, a bit clumsily but quickly enough.

Mike hops in after him.

'Sit there,' he says, pointing at the stern. Mike uses an oar to push the boat away from the rocks. When they're in more open water he pulls the oars in long steady strokes.

Anton can tell they're heading straight out into the harbour, and not for the far end of the foreshore, which is where he'd hoped they'd go. But why would they head out to the island? What's there? Contraband obviously. Cigarettes? Drugs? Guns? Anton doesn't want to get messed up in any of this. What if they're caught? What would happen to his grant? He'd psyched himself up for a little boat trip but now he's just sitting with nothing to do he starts to panic again.

It's okay, it's okay. It's just a boat. It's safe. A tsunami like the last one won't hit for another five hundred years at least. See. It's okay, statistics never lie.

But Anton knows very well that those telling the statistics often lie.

After an hour or so Mike stops rowing, having got to the southern side of Matiu Island. Anton can see the sweat pouring off him by the faint starlight. He assumes they're almost there.

'Your turn,' says Mike.

'My turn? I don't know how to row.'

'Your turn.'

Mike and Anton swap places. Mike leans forward and readjusts Anton's grip on the oars then sits back. He looks serious.

'Row,' he says.

There's something sinister about having to row, Anton thinks. Like making a condemned man dig his own grave.

Anton pulls back and forth for a minute until Mike leans forward and grabs the oars again.

'Put the oar down, like this, lean back and pull, then slide it up out of water, swing it back and slice down into the water again. Got it?'

Anton tries again, and it seems a bit better. Condemned men don't get lessons to make things easier he reassures himself. The water's calmer on this side of the island as it's sheltered from the northerly. Anton realises they're heading, not for the island but for the city. Maybe Mike's handed the oars over to him on this side because he can learn to row here without too much of a swell.

Anton rows. His wrists and knees feel weak, and his back and shoulder muscles burn. Mike is in the stern now, using a prop to steer as Anton doesn't seem to be able to coordinate himself well enough to keep going in a steady line. Yet. He can't help but feel a little pride well up. He's doing it. Not as strongly or as smoothly as Mike, sure, but he's rowing a boat, in the dark, across this harbour.

But the pride's short-lived as the wind hits them again and the waves get higher and sometimes an oar on one side doesn't enter the water at all and on the other side threatens to get sucked in. Mike leans over and grabs both oars and they manage to change places again.

'Take the rudder,' Mike shouts. Anton obeys though he's not sure exactly how to use it, but he soon gets the hang of it. They're heading, inexplicably, for where the CBD once was. Where will they be able to land?

The wind dies down by the time they finally make it across the harbour. Anton takes over the rowing again, though every muscle hurts. Mike's strong, but he must be exhausted. They get to the first remnant of a high-rise building as the full moon rises in the east.

The cliff faces of glass, leaning slightly, tower above them and continue down under the waves. The cool moonlight reflects off the glass and the water. Blue light, blue glass, blue water.

But as they glide past the next building the illusion of beauty's shattered, as every pane of glass has splintered and fallen, and the dark spaces beyond the reach of moonlight feel as though they're completely and utterly empty.

Anton shivers.

Mike leans over and stills his hands.

'You can stop.'

They float down what was once a city street, between glass and concrete precipices reaching up and out of the water high above them. The light flickers off the waves, off the reflections of waves in the windows.

'You haven't seen this before, I take it?' says Mike.

'No. No, I haven't. It's … well, it's horrific but also somehow beautiful.'

'It's not for the fainthearted, that's for sure.'

Anton wonders if that was a compliment. Mike gets comfortable and rolls a smoke.

'Best to come at the full moon. Best to see it looking *beautiful and horrific*, as you say. If you come in the daytime, it's just a fucken horror show.'

Mike puts the unlit rolly between his lips and takes over the rowing. Slowly now, resting between strokes, occasionally popping an oar into the water to correct his steering. They travel into the labyrinth of buildings. Anton was in the city, once, years ago when he had to visit the High Commission. But he doesn't recognise anything. Rows of gleaming facades extend out of the water at right angles where streets once were. They don't even look like streets anymore; they look like futuristic canals.

The two young men stop at an old masonry building, with ornate stone window surrounds and balconies on every floor. Anton can't see any broken windows, the French doors leading out onto each balcony seem to be perfectly aligned, and the only thing out of place is the barnacles now growing on the first-floor balcony where the tide sweeps in and out between the balustrades. The building across the road looks like it's reasonably new with the coloured panes of glass that were so in fashion just before the big one struck. It's pancaked, taking each successive floor with it as the top floor raced towards the ground. Anton shudders and turns back to look at the Victorian balcony Mike's tying the boat to.

Mike finishes an elegant knot then stands and heaves himself out of the water.

'Come on.'

Anton scrambles up, Mike pulling more than Anton can, his arms giving out, refusing to do anymore work. They slosh through a few inches of water, deeper into the building and just when Anton starts to freak out about how dark it's getting Mike turns on his headlamp. He opens a door and heads up a stairwell.

The building smells like the beach after a storm, like rotting seaweed and salt. They climb the stairs all the way to the top floor and come out into a large room with a view of the harbour, of Matiu Island, and the hill summit looming up in the distance behind.

'There used to be a bastard of a thing blocking the view just there,' says Mike pointing. 'But it collapsed, making that breakwater there. Quite handy, makes it reasonably calm here. Well, better than what it would have been otherwise. So, we can get in and out easily enough, as you saw.'

Mike unlocks the French doors, and they swing open freely. The two men step out into the moonlight.

Anton's still warm from the exertion of rowing, of climbing all the stairs, so he closes his eyes and lets the breeze wash over him. Opening his eyes, he looks up and down the canals and across the space opposite and to the north. He tries to imagine this as a typical city scene. He can see street signs just visible below the waterline, but can't read them from up so high, and it makes him feel a bit queasy, trying to think what it used to look like. He shakes his head. Looking at the moonlight reflecting off walls of glass it's a new world, a different one, one with an eerie beauty.

Mike puts down the large waterproof bag he put their daypacks in, unties it and tips all of their belongings on the ground. He fishes out a couple of sleeping bags.

'Rest up.' He points at a thin mattress lying on what was once a couple of office desks, pushed together to make a bedframe of sorts. Mike takes a similar one across the room, lies down and starts snoring within a couple of minutes. Anton takes off his wet clothes and slips into his sleeping bag naked, too tired to get changed into anything dry. He means to turn over to look at the harbour, but he too falls asleep and sleeps soundly.

Anton wakes to the sound of seagulls and the warmth of the sun shining on his face. Sitting up he squints and shields his eyes. The sun has just risen above the hill summit and shines directly across the office space to where he has, until a moment ago, been sleeping. What looked magical in moonlight now looks stark, desolate. The office is an open-plan space, grey dividers, grey desks, grey blinds, but most things have been pushed to the back leaving a wide-open space in front of the doors out to the balcony. Anton gets up and stretches his stiff arms and neck. He slips on a T-shirt and trousers then walks across to open the doors. The sound of the seagulls and the waves crashing into the buildings below echoes strangely up and down the manmade corridors.

'It's creepy, eh?'

Anton turns and sees Mike sitting up grimacing as he too stretches.

'I was thinking how I have a unique opportunity here. I'd like to go exploring if I may. Some of those other buildings look interesting.'

'No,' says Mike. Tone flat.

Anton is a little taken aback. Mike softens.

'Look, this one's clear. No one died here so this is where we sleep. I'll show you a few others later. Buildings that have been checked and blessed. And I don't care if you believe in that or not, you don't mess with it, right?'

Mike walks over and stands beside Anton and looks up and down the streets. They're at the corner of an intersection, a crossroads.

'It may look beautiful to you, but a lot of people died here. Luckily not so many as it was a Sunday night, so it could've been worse, much worse. But people we loved died here. Remember that. We don't come here for entertainment.'

'So, why are we here? Is it guns? I'm really not at all comfortable transporting guns, you know. I just need that to be said.' Anton sticks out his chin, teeth clenched.

Mike sprinkles tobacco that's threatening to fly away in the wind, looking up without raising his head, appraising Anton before licking the paper and looking down again to roll the smoke. He cups his hands and lights it before taking a long drag.

'Guns?'

Anton swallows. What else can it be? Explosives? He suddenly hopes it's guns after all.

Mike walks back inside, picks up his day pack, leaving the sleeping gear, and heads for the stairwell.

'Get the door, eh? Don't let those bloody seagulls in.'

Anton quickly closes the doors and pulls on his shoes. He still doesn't know what they're supposed to be doing here but he doesn't like the prospect of being left alone. It occurs to him that all the marble, all the granite and concrete make it look like an enormous graveyard. He runs across the room as the door to the stairwell slams closed.

The tide's gone out and there's no water on the first floor. Anton slips on some seaweed but regains his footing and gets to the balcony just as Mike unties the knot holding the boat in place. Anton gets in as Mike pushes off and grabs the rudder.

'Where to?'

Mike laughs.

'Thought you didn't want to have anything to do with ... with ... what's it we're doing again? Gun running?'

'I don't know.'

'You don't know. So why are you letting your imagination go crazy? Let your imagination go crazy and very soon you're going crazy, don't you know that?'

'I suppose I don't.'

'Look.' Mike stops rowing. 'If you're going to live in Awaawa you're going to have to learn how to survive. I don't want your death on my conscience.'

Is that a threat? It sounds like a threat. Mike seems too relaxed to be threatening him. But maybe he's a psychopath?

Mike rows down the street. Or what is it now? A seaway? A canal? They travel for five minutes until they get to what was once a narrow street that's now a fast-flowing stream of water. Mike ties the boat to what was the top of a kinetic sculpture. Anton can see the brightly coloured discs which once moved with the wind covered in barnacles and slime below water calmly moving with the swell.

'Hold her steady,' says Mike.

Anton holds onto the central pole of the sculpture as Mike grabs a rope and begins pulling in a fishing net.

A fishing net.

Anton closes his eyes in shame.

Mike pulls and pulls as more and more fish – some still alive, most dead – and more and more net, fill up the bottom of the boat. When done Mike grabs a rope strung between the buildings above them and pulls them along until the boat's next to a glass balcony and he jumps ashore, as it were, and leads the boat with Anton still in it up a narrow alleyway to a place where the boat can be tied up and unloaded easily. They pull the net out of the boat onto the balcony where the glass balustrades are missing and pluck all the fish out of the net. Mike smacks any wriggling fish over the head with a stick. Anton tries to take only the dead fish out but when he picks one up which starts to move furiously back and forth it slips from his hands. Mike grabs it before it slides back into the water, holds it down and passes the stick to Anton.

'Kill it.'

'I'm, ah, well—'

'If you want to eat you need to learn how to kill. Stop messing about and bloody well hit it.'

Anton smacks the fish in the head, but it just thrashes about more violently.

'Hit it!'

Anton closes his eyes and smacks it. When he opens his eyes, he sees the fish open mouthed as though it's just as surprised as he is.

Mike looks stern.

'It doesn't feel good killing stuff, eh?'

'No, it doesn't.'

'But if you want to eat you've got to kill. No getting around it. There're no supermarkets here for you to outsource the killing to someone else. So, make sure you don't let the thing suffer, and don't ever waste food, right?'

'I might try being vegetarian for a while.'

Mike snorts.

'Yeah right. You're going to make your own soy milk? Vegan cheese? Grow quinoa? Look around you. Do you see any of that stuff growing here? All that stuff needs importing. You want to be self-sufficient the first thing you've got to learn is what lives here, what grows here, and how to harvest, hunt, and kill.'

'Right. Ah, Mike?'

Mike resumes plucking fish out of the net.

'Yeah.'

'Is this why we're here?

Mike laughed.

'Why? Are you disappointed it's not gun running?'

'I do believe I owe you an apology. I thought badly of you.'

'No worries. And now for the fun bit.' Mike hands Anton a knife.

*

Once all the fish are gutted and salted Mike shows Anton how to thread a string through their gills and make a macabre type of dead-fish-bunting which he puts in two big plastic bags.

'Come on, we've got a bit of a climb.'

Mike lights a lantern and carries a bag of fish in one hand over his shoulder and lets the lantern dangle behind him lighting the way for Anton who's carrying the other bag. They climb and climb for ages. At what Anton thinks must be the top, they pause and catch their breaths.

'Halfway,' says Mike. It's hard to tell in the dim light, and Mike turns so quickly to resume climbing the stairs, but it looks like he's laughing.

Finally, when there are no more stairs to climb

Mike opens a door. The sudden brightness makes Anton shield his eyes. They're on the top floor of a very tall high-rise building. The floor slopes slightly upwards so most of the view's sky rather than harbour, and the morning sun floods the whole floor with light. Anton thinks for a second there's something sinister moving towards him, floating to meet him. Ghosts, ghouls, banshees. As his sight gets better, he sees fish hanging like streamers, corpses of animals hanging upside down.

'What is this place?'

'This is the *Majestic Larder*. All day sun and walls of glass so it's like an oven and I figured we're so high up there'd be no flies and it would make a brilliant place for making jerky and dried fish.' Mike sucks in air through his teeth. 'Fucken flies are everywhere though. At least those bastard stairs keep most thieves out. Here, give us a hand.'

They drag out long lines of fish and tie the ends of the string to hooks on the columns and filing cabinets seemingly put there for that purpose. When finished Mike folds the plastic bag up and takes the empty kete off his back and fills it with dry fish off the lines.

Anton walks up the slope to look out over the tops

of all the other buildings at the harbour, at the hills opposite. The high-rise buildings give way to twee wooden houses surprisingly close for what used to be a capital city. The houses look untouched from here. He thinks he sees washing on a clothesline. It almost looks normal, until he glances down the sharp slant of glass sliding right down into the water, where the water slops against the glass and he feels the floor move, the whole building sway violently side to side. He cries out, afraid he's about to skid down the cliff into the waters below.

Mike's there, pulling him back from the edge and shoving him roughly against a pillar, pinning him by the shoulders.

'Nothing's moving. Nothing's moving, eh? Close your eyes and put your hands on the column and tell your brain that.'

'It's an earthquake!'

'It's not a bloody earthquake, it's vertigo. Sorry, should have warned you. Now, tell yourself, nothing's moving. Nothing. Is. Moving. Alright?'

Mike lets go. Anton opens his eyes, feels his knees buckle, and is about to throw up.

'Come on,' says Mike. 'You're in control of this.

You just need to tell your brain to stop freaking out.'

Anton closes his eyes, rubs his face with his palms and takes a deep breath. He opens his eyes again and sees lines of fish suspended in the air, not moving, not swaying, but his mind tells him the building's lurching back and forth. Come on, he tells himself. Look at the evidence. Collect the data. Nothing's moving.

Things start to slow down. He studies the fish-bunting, steady, static. But the wavy lines on the blue carpet slop from side to side as though waves are washing over the floor. He decides to focus on the fish.

'I'm alright.'

Mike turns and resumes putting dried fish in the kete.

'About bloody time,' he says.

*

Down at water level again they get into the boat and make their way towards what looks like a main thoroughfare. When Anton tries to view the waterways as canals it's like a modern version of Venice. But when he recognises logos of particular chain stores, he sees the sunken city again and feels uneasy.

'You hungry?' says Mike.

'Yes, actually, now you come to mention it.'

'Pizza?'

'Surely you're joking?'

Mike says nothing but negotiates against the current down the canal and into an old arcade. They flatten their bodies against the bottom on the boat, only just fitting under an arch, and then are plunged into near darkness. The stairs of an escalator appear to be slowing rising but it's only the waves moving back and forth. Mike ties the boat to a balustrade, and they gingerly make their way up the steps and across a landing.

A faint light comes from under a door on the other side of the building and the unmistakable smell of pizza wafts towards them. Anton's stomach growls. Mike pushes open a door, and they walk into a brightly lit open-plan room full of mismatched office desks covered in tablecloths made from curtains. On each table there's an unlit candle stuck in an old wine bottle. Sunlight's streaming through a gap between piles of rubble on the opposite side of the street. There's about thirty people spread out around the room, swinging legs from office chairs, slowly rotating back and forth as they talk.

'Welcome to Ferruccio's,' says Mike. 'Sit here and don't let our stuff out of your sight.' He heads for what must be the kitchen.

After a minute, a young woman comes over and stands, hands in pockets, staring at Anton. She's dressed as though she's been out clubbing, heavy makeup and tired eyes. He's not sure what she wants so smiles nervously.

'Hi,' he says.

She raises her eyebrows and says something like 'Sup.' She looks and sounds bored by his presence but doesn't turn away.

'Well?' she says.

'Well, what?'

'Well, what do you want?'

'I don't want anything!'

'What the fuck are you doing here then? Order something or get out.'

'I … ahh …'

Just then Mike comes back with two beers.

'Hey Trish.'

'Mike.' Trish raises her eyebrows and crosses her arms.

'What's got your knickers in a twist?'

Trish nods at Anton.

'Oh, he's alright. He's with me. Trish, Anton. Anton, Trish.'

Trish nods and almost smiles at Anton. 'Sorry, if I'd known you were with Mike I wouldn't have been such a bitch.'

'Yes, you would've,' says Mike as he sits down.

'Fuck you.'

'Yes, please. Here or out back?'

Trish grunts and starts to walk away.

'Bring us pizza, bitch! Meat lovers!'

'There's no meat, dickhead,' she says over her shoulder. 'It's fish or nothing.'

'Oh, isn't there?' says Mike quietly.

Trish spins round and heads back.

'What have you got.'

She no longer sounds bored or defensive. She looks at Mike in a way that makes Anton feel uncomfortable, and a little jealous if he's honest with himself.

Mike kicks his backpack towards her.

'I know you love a bit of meat. Help yourself.'

Trish picks up the bag and weighs it admiringly,

nods and walks towards the kitchen.

'Watch the bags, eh,' Mike says to Anton as he jumps up to follow her.

Anton drinks his beer and although adamant he will wait for Mike, only a minute after the pizza arrives, he starts eating alone. The hot cheese! The fatty salami!

He's eaten more than half before he notices and stops. Appalled at his behaviour he tries to apologise as soon as Mike appears again, but Mike just waves away the apology and takes a slice.

'Greedy bastard,' he laughs.

*

Anton helps Mike load up the boat. It's full of bags that Mike has picked up from the pizzeria which seems to double as a trading post of sorts. Anton's worried about how low the boat sits in the water but says nothing. Mike rows with long deep strokes and they're soon heading back across the harbour as the sun heads across the sky.

'Shouldn't we go at night, so we can't be seen?' says Anton.

'By the snipers, you mean?'

'What?'

Mike laughs. 'We go with the tides and the weather.'

'Why did we come here in such a storm then?'

Mike stared at Anton for a moment then snorted.

'Storm? That was no storm. Shit mate, you're going to have to harden up if you're going to last long around here.'

Anton swallows and resolves to *harden up* as it were. It's a long way back, but he's not so scared on the return trip. When he starts to feel panicky, he closes his eyes like he did in the *Majestic Larder* and tells himself it's okay. And then surprisingly it is. Well, mostly. It's better, at least. They take turns rowing and that too seems easier in a way, but his muscles are still burning by the time they near the shore.

They drag the boat ashore and stow it in the bush and then carry the cargo up further. Anton's about to collapse. He tries to find the words to express his doubts about his ability to physically continue, as much as he wants to, feels compelled to. Just as he's about to speak Mike stops and drags a heavy plastic bag out from under some ferns. He pulls out a tarp and slings it over a branch to create a sloping wall stopping the worst of the southerly.

'We sleep here,' he says.

Anton says nothing. Just drops the bags and collapses on the ground where the tarp meets the ferns. Mike comes back a few minutes later, arms full of long ponga fronds to make a bed, to find Anton sound asleep. He stands for a moment trying to decide whether to kick Anton to move over or let him be. Instead, he lays the ferns beside him, yanks the sleeping bags out, unzips one and places it over Anton before climbing into his own.

Anton dreams of being in a boat rolling from side to side, that then somehow becomes a cradle and Marie's face appears singing a lullaby, *We will, we will, rock you*. Over and over.

Anton wakes with a start. The sound of the sea crashing on the beach below and a bird singing on a branch close to him is unexpected. He wonders where he is when a little blue penguin waddles past his face. He doesn't move but follows it with his eyes as it scrabbles noisily over the leaf litter, the ferns, the branches, then disappears from view.

'Was that—?'

'A kororā? Yup. They make nests in the bush,

under houses, in the cliffs.'

Anton rolls over to see Mike sitting upright.

'I've never seen a penguin before.'

'Thought you were some sort of bird expert?'

'Yes, well, no, not really. My research specialises in birds, so I suppose I am. Kind of.'

Mike looks at Anton as though he's an unfamiliar species of fish he's pulled out of his net.

'Actually, if I'm to be perfectly honest, I don't much like birds.'

'You don't like *birds*? You flew halfway around the planet to study something you don't even like? Why bother?'

'Well, ah, I wanted to travel. Thought it might be nice to come to a Pacific island. And, well, you've got lots of birds here …' Anton rubs his hands on his arms, trying to warm them. He starts to get up.

'Nah, stay still,' says Mike. 'If you're lucky you'll get breakfast in bed.'

'I beg your pardon?' says Anton.

A hand reaches over Anton's right shoulder holding a cup, surprising Anton enough to spill some of it.

'Careful, careful, hot hot hot,' says Tim.

'Tim!' Anton doesn't know if he's more surprised or happy to see Tim. He takes the cup.

'Yes, yes, Tim, Tim.' Tim pours another cup from a thermos and hands it to Mike.

'Ta mate.'

The three men sit quietly and drink strong, sweet coffee.

'Did you see? Did you see? What did you see?' says Tim to Anton. He's wide-eyed like an excited kid.

'What did I see? Oh, I saw the *Majestic Larder*, there was a tremendous number of steps to get up there, the pizza shop, we met a young lady named Trish. The *canals* were great. It's like a space-age city, futuristic walls of glass rising up out of the sea. I'd heard the city had sunk but I never imagined how beautiful it would be ...' Anton trails off as he sees the confusion on Tim's face.

Mike has stood up and folded the tarp and stuffed it in a bag and then back under the ferns. He sighs as he packs his sleeping bag.

'He means wildlife,' he says to Anton then turns to Tim.

'There were dolphins in the harbour entrance, half a dozen or so, quite far off. Loads of stingrays, all sizes, including Mr Scar-back himself. Maybe an orca, I only saw a glimpse of movement out of the corner of my eye, could've been a dolphin, on the far side of the island. Jellyfish in the canals, the ones with pink circles, and loads of bluebottles, some dead on the steps to Ferruccio's. Chaffinches of course, starlings, blackbirds. The tūī were fighting like fury. The young gulls are nesting on the balconies, and there are still quite a few rock pigeons around, they're found the pizza shop – Trish is having a hell of a job keeping them and the sparrows out. She said there are a couple of kororā nesting in the old AA building, but I didn't see any apart from that little fella that went up here just now.' Mike signals the direction the penguin went with an unlit cigarette.

Anton couldn't add anymore information if he tried. He didn't notice any of the creatures Mike's mentioned. Mike's words about being a bird expert are still ringing in his ears. If he can't even report back on wildlife, and he can't do any of the practical tasks needed, what use is he?

'Oh,' says Mike. 'And there were sandpipers on the beach that we disturbed when heading out. They were saying something I couldn't quite catch, like, *Get out!*

or *Get help!* Something like that.'

Tim laughs. He rifles through his pack and pulls out hard-boiled eggs still in their shells, slightly stale rye bread, and small, hard, bitter, green apples. As they eat Mike stops at intervals to scrape what looks like dandruff from his stubble onto his peeled egg. Anton wonders what it is before absent-mindedly scratching the beginnings of his own beard and feeling the dried salt coming off on his fingers. He too sprinkles the salt onto the eggs, making them taste sharper, better. Afterwards he puts a hand through his hair to comb it and finds clumps of hair like straw, refusing to part into individual strands. He desperately wants a bath or even a shower and doesn't even care if it's not hot.

Tim's plucking breadcrumbs from his shirt and popping them into his breast pocket. Anton can't fathom why until he sees a beak and feathered head dart out, take a crumb, and disappear back into the depths of the flannel shirt.

'What on earth?' exclaims Anton.

'Starlight,' says Tim. 'Starlight, star bright, starlings are star bright.'

Mike throws a bag towards Anton.

'Come on, let's get going.' More of a command

than a suggestion.

They pack up, dividing the load more manageably between the three of them.

As Anton puts his pack on his back, he marvels at how energised he feels, despite the sore muscles, and sleeping on the hard earth. Heading into the valley the second time in less than a week he's amazed at how much has happened and how he feels like he's heading *home*.

'So, you'd like bacon and eggs for breakfast, every morning, eh?' says Mike.

'Oh, that was quite unexpected and a most wonderful breakfast the other day. Thank you. But now I do understand that's not the usual state of affairs.'

'So … you wouldn't say no to having it more often then?'

'I certainly would not. That would be splendid. If it was at all possible.'

'Of course it's possible.' Mike lifts some ferns off the ground to uncover a couple of rifles. He hands one to Anton. 'Right. So, you'll take that with you when you head up into the hills.'

'That's a gun!'

'Very observant. A .303 to be precise.'

'I couldn't possibly do anything with that!'

'How else are you going to get the pig for the bacon? Doesn't grow on trees, you know. You sitting under the trees being all quiet while you watch your birds is perfect for pig hunting. Though, if you see a deer or goat don't be shy, eh?'

'I'm terribly sorry but I don't think I'd be able to bring myself to do it.'

Mike stands square in front of him, one rifle cradled in the crook of his arm, the other held out like you'd hold a dead rabbit by its ears.

'You met Komas at the street party, right? Zara's husband?'

'I think so, briefly, yes.'

'I've got a lot of time for Komas. Seems a bit meek at first, perhaps? Quiet, stern. But he's solid. He's from Iraq originally. Kurdish. Lived for a long time up in their mountains fighting against Saddam's soldiers. He was starving one time, hadn't eaten for days and a pig walked past, so he took his gun and shot it, cooked it, and ate it. That's why some of the others from that neck of the woods won't talk to him. They say it's forbidden, and he should've died. Said as much at a street barbeque once. Hell of a standoff. But Komas stood his ground and said no. He stood there and said that as a father, and as a husband, his duty was to stay alive so he could return home to his family, to provide for them, and to protect them. So, he ate the pig. I reckon if he can do that, if he can risk offending his god, his family, his neighbours, and himself, then the likes of you, who actually enjoys a plate of bacon, can do it too.'

Anton swallows hard and takes the gun gingerly.

'I'm not giving you the ammo though until you've had some practice, eh? Carry it like this,' Mike adjusts Anton's grip. 'And you don't ever point it at anything unless you mean to kill it. You don't fire unless you have a clean shot. I don't want to hear that you've injured some poor beast and it's run off into the bush to die a painful death.'

'I really—'

Mike cuts him off. 'Lesson number one. You carry this pointed down, even when unloaded. Always think safety. Once you can do that consistently I'll arrange some shooting lessons for you. Tui's the second best shot in the valley. She might give you lessons. She might not too, she's a hard bitch. But don't tell me you want bacon and eggs for breakfast and then not be willing to do the hard yards to get it, alright?'

'Who's the best shot?'

Mike rolls his eyes, salutes then grabs his own pack and heads up the track leaving Anton holding a gun for the first time in his life and never having felt more vulnerable.

*

Marie has straightened up Anton's room, put doilies under objects, a couple of larger doilies under the laptop, and a small vase of flowers on the desk. Anton frowns. He had laid out his papers on the desk and floor in a pattern that made sense to him but obviously looked like a mess because Marie has collected them all into one neat pile, edges parallel with the edge of the desk.

He sighs as he sorts through them, putting them into order, pages overlapping in places to indicate a connection with another pile. What he really needs is a big noticeboard with multicoloured drawing pins and bits of string. The other doctorate students he's shared an office with called it *Anton's murder board*

153

which was a tad sinister he thought. He does like a big space, though, where he can move bits of paper around as he tries to get the whole picture into his mind.

He's tired. But hopeful. He seems to have passed some sort of initiation test and can now get on with his research. He's behind already, but it's still early days. He picks up his bag to leave.

There's a knock on the door. It's opened, before he can say anything, by Marie who's standing unwinding a scarf from her hair.

'You're back then! You gave me a bit of a turn the other morning when you weren't here. Thought you'd gone to the outhouse and fallen down the hole!'

Marie laughs at her own joke. Anton fidgets.

'Good morning, Marie. I'm terribly sorry to have left in such a manner, I hope it was no bother.'

'No bother at all my love. Now, did you get the blessing you were after?'

'The blessing?'

'From the man on the hill? You said as much in your note.'

'The note? Oh, yes, the note …'

'Yes, love. So, did you get it? The blessing? It's pretty important, isn't it, before you go into the bush.'

Anton holds his breath a moment, thinking of what to say. 'He wasn't home. I thought I'd try again today.'

'Wasn't home'? Marie looks at him, eyebrows raised high and it's only now he realises she's shaved them off and drawn them back on again. Have they always been like that? Surely, he'd have noticed. He stares for longer than he should.

'No, not home.'

'That doesn't sound right, love. Are you sure you got the right place?'

'Maybe I went to the wrong house?'

'Wrong house? I would think so if you went to a house at all, my love. Pete doesn't live in a house as such. And he's *always* home.'

'Right. So, I'll pop in on my way back from the bush.'

'You can't just go into the bush without a blessing, love. Why don't you go see Mike now and sort it all out?' She tips her head back and holds her arm out far from her body looking at her watch. 'He should still be down the pub.'

Anton's supervisor warned him not to upset the locals, to abide by local customs, not to mess things up for future research projects. Marie's staring at his bag of gear. He feels obliged to put it down on the floor.

'Right,' he says as he walks past Marie and tries to look casual as he grabs an apple from the fruit bowl on the kitchen table. 'I'll go see Mike now, see where I went wrong.' He rushes out the door not waiting for Marie to question him any longer. He doesn't notice as he puts the apple in his pocket that he's grabbed one of the wax pieces of fruit Marie keeps in the bowl to make it look more plentiful, more cheerful, like the good old days.

'Now, what in the dickens does he want one of those for?' Marie says to herself as she watches Anton hurry down the garden path.

*

There's always been one pub in town and post-earthquake there's been no change. People surprised at there being only one pub in a town like Awaawa are people who don't belong to darts clubs, bowls clubs, league clubs, working men's clubs, and therefore don't know about the considerable number of members-only drinking establishments. Mike, however, has always been a pub man, not liking the pretence surrounding sports clubs where some members never once partake in sport. He also likes the odd game of darts. Something that never takes place in the local darts club.

The local tavern was originally named The Flying Juggernaut. A grand sign, spray-painted by a group of talented young PEP workers back in the eighties, was over a metre high and the length of the building, which although impressively sized was only just long enough for such a grand name in large lettering. The lettering has suffered through the hot summers and frosty winters of Awaawa. Those over in Hill Valley ridicule the cold winters in the valley, much cooler than in Hill Valley, perhaps because it's only locals who know, or care to acknowledge, that it's also much hotter in the summer. Or perhaps they like to keep it to themselves, a treasured secret that keeps them warm in their hearts when the scorn's poured on.

Over the years the paint's cracked and peeled, it's been vandalised over, and repainted with brushes held by less skilful artists. The whole panel at the end blew off in that storm five years back and barely missed Mr Henderson's head as he popped over the road to check on / do away with / tie up the roses of her-over-the-road. The last panel was never recovered, well, not by the tavern staff. Rumour has it that it became the wall of Mrs Henderson's new potting shed but no one likes to ask her in case it sounds like an accusation. So, since then, the sign's said, 'The Flying Jug'. And that's, let's be honest, a far more fitting name.

Ava stands behind the bar, looking the worse for wear. She did an all-nighter at the darts club, not playing any darts of course, but it's always open until the early hours. Afterwards she went to Darren's place round the corner, where there was still some homebrew from the party last week. And now, here she is at work looking like shit and scaring away any customers that aren't familiar with her look, or in other words no one, since no one who's not a regular drinks here.

Except Anton.

So, here he comes, looking like a speck of shit on an ice cream, and knowing full well that no matter how he phrases it, how polite or casual or friendly or cool he tries to sound, the moment he opens his mouth he's fucked.

'Good morning.'

Nothing in return. A look. Of disgust? Maybe Ava just feels nauseous, and Anton shouldn't be so fucking paranoid.

'Mike?' he says. 'Is he around, by any chance?'

There's a couple of guys at the bar looking equally the worse for wear. One of them turns and looks Anton up and down like he's a letter from an insurance company.

'Look around you, dipshit. Does it look like anyone else is here?'

Ava sniffs, shelves the glass she's been drying. 'Let him be, Gary.' She glances at Anton. 'Try the lounge, honey.'

Anton apologises, shuffles backwards, almost makes a run for the door but manages the long walk from the bar to the other side where the lobby is, passing the doors to the men's and women's toilets when Mike comes out, adjusting his fly.

'Mike!'

'Yeah, what's up?'

'I was, um …' Anton hears laughter from behind him. Nothing to do with Anton actually but something snaps. 'Isn't it a bit early to be drinking!'

He's had enough. Why should he have to get

permission to do serious work from a bunch of drunkards?

Mike pats him on the shoulder. 'Come on, we've got work to do.' He walks through the lounge doors and Anton can do nothing but follow along behind him like an orphaned lamb.

The lounge is full of smoke, of varying odours, and pints of, not lager, but not stout either. Something cloudy. It doesn't look like particularly good beer. Mike holds out a pint glass to Anton, who shakes his head.

'I'd rather not, if you don't mind.'

'*I* mind,' says Mr Henderson.

Mike continues to hold out the glass. He nods in Mr Henderson's direction.

'He's the finest kombucha brewer in the valley. Best not to be rude, eh?'

Anton takes the glass, eyes down, smiling sheepishly. He takes a sip.

'Oh, it's lovely.'

Mr Henderson grunts and turns away. A man Anton doesn't know resumes talking.

'So anyway, their idea is to barricade the hill road and stop the inspectors coming in. Inspectors, police, government officials, anyone they don't like essentially.'

'Good!' says Bill.

'Except that'll include anyone bringing in meat, leather, synthetic fibres, anything they don't approve of,' says Mike.

'I don't care so much about that,' says Bill, 'so much as the fact that all those good for nothings will be standing around protesting and expect someone else to feed them.'

'Keep the valley for the locals,' says Mr Henderson. 'Who are all these outsiders coming in? Get rid of the lot of them, I say.' He glances at Anton. 'No offence.'

'Point is,' resumes the original speaker, 'we need to stop these idiots. We're all so damned busy just trying to stay alive we don't have time to protest the protests.'

'Why do we need to stop them? Let them waste their time if they want,' says a woman at the end of the bar.

'Because,' says Mike, 'it takes a shit load of work to grow a few veggies, hunt down a deer, catch some fish. They want us all to pool our resources for redistribution without contributing themselves.'

'They're taking all the government food parcels for

themselves,' says Mr Henderson.

'You said you didn't want a government handout,' says Bill. 'Make up your mind.'

'Don't see why those lazy buggers should get it. If the damned government stopped sending in aid all those bastards would piss off and leave us to it. Never done a good day's work in their lives, not one of them. Not even for a minute.'

Mike clears his throat. 'My concern is the idea that they want a meat free zone. We need to hunt. Not just for the food, but to counter the pests in the area.'

'You're not going to be supporting that bloody fool Derek *Hopeless*, are you? Him and his madcap extended bird sanctuary idea.'

'Look I'm not too keen on most of his ideas but the sanctuary idea might help. It'll protect the birds, but it could also stop the government giving the land over to developers for housing.'

'But we need housing!'

'Sure, we need housing, but *we* won't get any of the houses. They'll give great big swathes of land to the developers and then the original locals won't be able to afford any of them.'

'My house's alright,' says the original man.

'No, it's not. Sunshine Construction have their beady eyes on that area. The council will up the rates till you can't pay anymore, seize your land, bulldoze your house, and build ten town houses in its place.'

'Bloody bastards! I'd like to see them try!'

'Look what's happened over the hill. They confiscated all the land and said it'd be turned back into market gardens. But what have they done? Gave it to one farming conglomerate and mark my words they'll find some way to build on it at some point in the future. And not little family businesses like us. We won't get the contracts.'

'Listen, let's consider the idea of an extended sanctuary,' says Mike. 'It'll keep the bush and birds intact, and that might be enough to keep us on as custodians.'

'Is that why he's here?' Henry points at Anton.

Mike nods.

'Anton might be able to provide us with some data to convince them to leave the bush alone and not bulldoze it. Developers will say it's to house the homeless in eco-friendly houses but they're destroying bird habitat for rich clients. We need to prove it's a sham.'

'Is that true?' Mr Henderson says to Anton. 'Can you help?'

Anton swallows hard, 'Ahhh, well, I'm not sure that I—'

Mike rests a hand on Anton's shoulder.

'He can show that we've managed to keep small populations of whitehead, stitchbird and weka alive, and that the deer-proof fence and pest control has made a huge difference in numbers even outside of the sanctuary. If we could get a predator-proof fence imagine how amazing the birdlife would be.'

A young man with long hair tied into a bun had walked into the room and stood listening.

'Deer are beautiful animals; you shouldn't stop them from making their homes in the forest.'

'They kill the trees the birds need for food,' says Mike. 'Deer, pigs, and goats are pests that we need to focus on, the ones that need culling—'

'Meat is murder!' a woman behind him shouts.

'Murderer!' screams the young man.

Half the bar start yelling at once, across the room.

'Oh, for fuck's sake,' says Mike. He turns and tugs on Anton's elbow, showing they should head for the door.

They're followed out by Tui and Jay. As they cross the car park Ava, who's having a smoko break on the back steps, sees them, and comes to join them.

They stop at a large golden Ford. Mike slips out some keys, unlocks it and they all get in. Anton tries to insist that Ava get in before he does, holding the door open, but she gives him such a look of disgust he gets in the middle back seat.

Anton's surprised but happy at the prospect of a drive. He looks forward to seeing the other end of the valley perhaps. But they don't seem to be going anywhere.

Tui's furious.

'Stupid fuckers, why can't they—'

Anton unintentionally starts speaking at the same time.

'I was wondering, that is to say—'

Both stop and Tui turns around, eyebrows raised, surprised at his audacity for daring to speak at all. But he's started and senses that it might be better to keep going, change the subject, play dumb, hope for the best.

'Marie says I had to see Pete. Who's he?'

'Pete?' says Jay. 'You haven't heard of Pete yet? He's

only the best bloody surfer there is. He rode the wave all the way up the valley, over the roads and the cars, the houses and the farmland, over the bodies of his family and friends. He rode the wave that was more tree trunks and tractor tyres, leaves and litter, synthetic oil and topsoil, than it was water.'

'Don't make it sound so fucken heroic,' says Ava. 'Think what an experience like that does to a man.'

'Makes him an oracle! A miracle! A seer of sounds.' Jay slaps the back of the car seat for emphasis.

'Wouldn't that make him a hearer, not a seer? says Anton.

There's silence in the car. Jay and Ava in the backseat edge slightly closer to the doors. Mike's in the driver's seat, and therefore the one with the power, the power to use the rear vision mirror and see without moving the head. Even now, with no petrol, no roads, nowhere to go, no key in the ignition, the sedan seating/pecking order is this: driver's seat, front passenger seat, left rear seat, right rear seat, then that little seat in the middle with the lap belt. Not that anyone wears seatbelts anymore, or ever did (we're talking about the occupants of an early Ford Falcon after all) but that's the seat that comes last. It's not the last place someone can be, it's the last seat. And it's pretty far down there in desirable places to be, but the boot's another place.

Don't be fooled by Hollywood movies. Boots aren't just spaces for dead bodies and hostages to be placed, they're legitimate places for riding in a car, due to the solitude provided if you're shy, the personal space if you're freaking out, the not needing to share a smoke, the lesser threat of mistakenly brushing up against one of the bodies either side and being called a fag or a lemon.

Though, some think the boot's less desirable than even the little seat in the middle with the lap belt. Ava says the middle seat's better than the boot any day. But that's because she was trapped in a car one time that had crashed and there were dripping bodies and screaming bystanders, and no one thought to see if the passenger in the boot was okay. Some people don't know the pecking order of seating and don't think to look in the boot when they find a car crashed.

There's also the back of the ute or van or station wagon under a blanket in case the road pirates stop the car and see an unsecured passenger and are looking to give the driver a ticket. *Unsecured passenger* usually means Tim, but not always. At least in a crash the body will be flung about in a way that means it'll be found sooner, be saved, or be buried. Whether the place is better or worse than the boot depends entirely on the state of the blanket. But we won't go into that now, use your imagination, as this car, on this day, has no blanket, and no one in the boot.

Though if Anton keeps asking stupid questions or making stupid comments, he might just end up there, if only for old time's sake.

Ava looks straight at Anton, albeit without turning her head.

'He's a seer, alright?'

Eyebrows raised in the reflection of the rear vision mirror. Tongue pressed firmly against the roof of the mouth. Bodies pressed against the rear doors. A yearning for the days when a moving car meant the driver could take a corner too fast to teach those in the back a lesson, or in the winter put the windows all the way down and lock them, or put the kiddy-locks on the doors. But raised eyebrows in the rear vision mirror still have the power to instil fear, especially in those who know the havoc caused by a driver's recently freed jandal being swished wildly round with one arm while the other holds onto the steering wheel. Ahh, the good old days.

Anton doesn't know about such things, a shortcoming not entirely of his own doing of course, but a shortcoming, nonetheless. He does, however, possess the power of knowing when to shut the fuck up.

Sometimes.

He's fairly inconsistent in this.

If there was petrol, they'd continue on down the road. But the car's now just a nostalgic meeting point out of the worst of the cold, out of the biting rain and the wind, a place where the younger adults can meet but avoid eye contact; sit but avoid cups of tea being thrust into their hands; escape, even if only in their minds.

Mike grips the steering wheel as though navigating a difficult turn.

'Yeah, you need to see Pete. But we might all need to go see him, actually, after today's performance in there.'

The occupants of the car start to disagree but it's Anton's voice that wins out.

'Look, it's all very nice of you to introduce me to

this *man on the hill*, is it?' he says. 'But I've got to get on, data to collect, research to be done ...'

'Yeah, about that,' says Mike.

'I don't need any help, really, thank you.'

'Yeah, that's good cause we're not really here to help so much as to make sure you follow the rules.'

'Rules?'

'Rules. Procedures. Protocol. Law of the land. You need to see Pete first.'

A starling lands on the bonnet of the car and stares at them through the glass.

'I need permission. Is that it? From whom?'

Mike points down the valley. 'You need to see the man on the hill first. He can help. Don't worry, we'll arrange it all. But you need to see him first.'

'Well, let's go then.'

'Shall we drive?' says Mike turning to face Anton.

Anton's not sure if it's a question or if they're all silently laughing at him, so he says nothing. Just stares back, heartbeat pounding in his ears.

Mike turns to the front and taps on the glass in front of the starling.

'Yeah, well, here's the thing. It's a bit of a trek,' says Mike. 'Need to prepare. Why don't you go help Marie with some preserving, she'd like that, and we'll get back to you when it's time.'

Mike slaps the steering wheel, the universal signal to depart and they all leap out. All except Anton. He can't move. Trapped in a prison of his own making, he discovers he did up the seat belt automatically when he sat down, even now, even here, he did it without thinking and he's left by himself in the car. The others wait without talking. Some things are just too fucken tragic even to take the piss out of.

When he finally extracts himself from the vehicle, he sees Tim arrive, lift the starling from the windshield, and pop it in his pocket.

Anton's about to comment on it when he's distracted by Mike's words.

'Right, Tim. Listen. You and Anton, you'll be with me tomorrow. Tui, you check routes and dates. Make sure you get the suspicious days and times—'

'*Auspicious* ...' says Tui quietly.

'Auspicious days and times. Ava, you gather supplies from the olds. Meet at the Holden this time tomorrow.'

'Tim?'

'Yes, yes?'

'We're going over the hill to get an offering, okay. But listen. You're not to fuck around over there, wandering off. We're getting an offering. That's all. You up for that?'

Tim picks at the dirt under his nails.

'Timmy Tim Tim!'

'Okay, okay.'

Small voice. Joy sucked out of it. A voice with no breath.

Half the inhabitants of Kōwhai Grove seem to be crammed into Marie's kitchen where they're all shelling broad beans at the kitchen table. As soon as Anton walks in he's given a pinny and a large, ancient plastic bowl and more broad beans than he's seen in his life.

'They say the man on the hill lives on the very spot where the waves deposited him. Where he landed, he stayed, built shelter, and sits there still. Waiting for another wave.' Marie nods to herself, dropping beans into her bowl. 'Telling all who seek his wisdom what waves will come into their lives.'

There's nods of heads and murmurs of agreement and the sound of beans hitting the sides of bowls.

'Except …' says Doris. 'Well … the wave can't have got him up there. It's too high.'

'Too high? Too high?' Garunda almost shouts as he tears at the bean shells. 'Don't you remember how high that wave was? Enormous! Never seen such a thing. Hope I never see the likes of it again!'

'Of course, I remember, I'm not as doddery as all that. But the wave would have gotten smaller by the time it got up the valley.'

'No, dear, it was ever so big,' says Zara.

'I heard he was standing on the rise coming up to the old Pencarrow lighthouse,' says Andira. 'I went there once on a school trip with the kids. They say he was standing on the ridge when the wave came up to exactly that height and gently lifted him off the ground and he surfed up the valley on a piece of four by two.'

'I don't believe a piece of four by two would be there,' says Mr Henderson. 'It's farmland around the lighthouse. Not a building in sight.'

'Maybe he was repairing the lighthouse?' says Zara.

'Why? No one uses it anymore,' says Garunda as he slams bean shells onto the table.

'Well, I don't know,' says Andira, throwing the beans into her bowl so hard they bounce right out again. 'That's what I heard. How else would he get so far up the valley?'

'I heard he surfed on the back of a stingray,' says Doris.

'No one could have surfed that wave,' says Garunda. 'It destroyed everything. There's nothing left of Petone, and you want to say he surfed up the valley? Of all the half-baked ideas I've heard in my time — '

'Yeah. He did!' says little Danny popping up from under the table where he's supposedly shelling beans but has a suspiciously green stain around his mouth. 'He was on top of the wave. Petone was underneath it. And he surfed like this!' Danny stretches out his arms and wobbles on the blue lino.

'Wasn't he surfing out at Bluff Point? Where the sewer outlet is,' says Marie. 'It would make more sense if he surfed up on an actual surfboard.'

'Yeah,' says Tim. 'Yeah, yeah, yeah. Bluff point. Great surfing there. Great surfing, good waves, good waves.'

'Great diarrhoea too, I bet,' says Anton. Absentmindedly. Almost to himself. Intended for himself alone.

They've forgotten he's there despite him being the

one to raise the topic of Pete. Everyone except Tim stops shelling beans to look intently at Anton. He really doesn't get it, does he? Hopefully, his mother loves him for no one else ever will if he keeps this up.

Feeling the stare Anton figures he might as well speak up. 'So, let me get this right,' he says as he finishes shelling a pod. 'This guy surfed up the valley on the crest of the great wave and where the wave set him down, he made his home. And now everyone in the valley goes to see him because supposedly, somehow, that's made him wise?'

There's incredulity in Anton's voice that he means for the story of the wave, but they hear it as doubting the existence of great wisdom.

There's always been great wisdom in the valley. Wisdom, believed, recognised, by few outside these hills. Wisdom spoken by the young and the unemployed. Murmured by the insomniacs. Muttered by the maniacs. Spluttered by the drunks at the tavern. Shouted by the husbands in the garages. Whispered by the kids quietly smoking behind them. The incessant nattering in our ears by those who won't let something like death stop them from handing out advice.

Wise words have always been available in the

valley for those who want to listen. There're wise words there now, too, but it's only the hunting of rare objects, the bearing of them to the hut on the hill halfway down the valley to the sea, and the listening to Pete's words in the smoky darkness that makes their message audible, meaningful. It's the bottle of beer, the bushwhacking, all the bother that makes the message worth hearing. If they were on the radio, the wise words, no one would even bother turning up the volume.

Mike appears at the backdoor. Or rather Mike speaks from where he's propping up the door frame. Goodness knows how long he's been there.

'Yes, Anton,' says Mike. 'That's right and if you need an answer to a question, need help on your quest, then you've got to pay Pete a visit.'

'Well, I don't really have a question.'

'You don't have any birds, do you? And you need birds for your research.'

'Oh, well, yes, but if I just—'

'If you just go and talk to Pete you'll have birds, won't you?' says Marie smiling.

There're mutters of agreement around the table and Anton nods. In silence. He doesn't agree. It's more a nod of acknowledgment, of hearing words swirl round the cartilage of his ear. Even Anton knows that if you stay silent people will just assume you've said what they want you to say. Anton makes no commitment one way or the other.

*

Mike looks across the T-junction and straight down Patterson Street sloping gently to the sea.

Nothing. No cars. No people, no … well, nothing to cause any concern.

The house has a couch on the veranda. It makes him smile. For a while there, couches began disappearing as houses were bought up, done up, flicked on, knocked down, replaced. He'd grown up with couches on verandas. The Greys had never gotten rid of a couch. Couches just migrated from lounge to veranda to carport to the end of the garden. There'd always been somewhere to sit, or to sleep. Always someone sitting, sleeping, to shake and bum a smoke off.

Beats sitting on the cold wooden steps of most of the remaining houses. Especially here, where he can see the water flat and green in front of the dark blue peak of Matiu Island, and the cumulus clouds of greys and whites and pinks over the harbour entrance.

He carefully lays the pouch of tobacco on his knee, pulls out some papers, and makes a narrow, but not too narrow, line. He lifts it to lick along the edge of the paper when his hands jerk upwards just enough to dislodge the tobacco onto his lap but not enough to lose the paper. So, he sits, his tongue halfway out, frozen, about to lick an empty paper.

Breathe. Breathe.

His peripheral vision tells him she's beside him. She came down the side of the house and stands staring at him. He berates himself for being off-guard, for letting the joy of having a rest, of looking at the view and having a smoke, for distracting him from the mission.

Breathe.

He moves his eyes without turning his head and then slowly lets his head follow until he's staring straight into her face.

His nostrils fill with the earthy smell of her.

Mike's on the veranda a good couple of feet above the ground, with a wooden balustrade between him and her. He's safe. That's what he tells himself. He's safe. She can't trample him. But it's not being trampled that frightens him. It's inexplicable why she scares him so bloody much.

Suddenly there's a noise from behind him as a sash window is jerked upwards. The cow startles as Tim climbs out.

'Go on love, love go on, off you go, off you go,' says Tim as he pats her backside.

Anton leans out the window and watches.

The cow grunts and saunters through what was once the front garden and off towards the harbour.

Mike still has his hands raised up to his chin holding an empty ciggy paper.

'Mike doesn't like cows,' says Tim. 'Mike might not like. No, no, no. Scary, too scary.'

'Shut the fuck up, Tim,' says Mike quietly.

But Tim does not shut up.

'Cows' eyes,' says Tim slowly, staring intently at Anton, 'look like sharks' eyes!'

Anton can't help himself.

'I did read somewhere that more cows kill people each year than sharks.'

Tim's eyes widen, his mouth hangs open, and he

nods vigorously.

'Yes! Yes, yes, yes.'

Mike sinks down into the couch and carefully slides the ciggy paper back in the cardboard sheath. He picks the strands of tobacco off his jeans one by one and places them back in the pouch.

'Alright, what did you find?' he says. Gruffly.

'Clothes!' says Tim. 'Clothes, clothes, lots of clothes. Need a T-shirt? New shirt? Long-sleeved? Short-sleeved? Short shorts, shoes, scarf, scarf, socks?'

Mike sighs.

'Go on then.'

Tim jumps on the railing, steps across what was once the boundary between the two houses to the window sash and swings inside. Anton gingerly follows him and upstairs they grab armfuls of clothes and throw them down from the upstairs bedroom onto the neighbour's veranda.

Once they're all downstairs again Tim holds up the items one by one while Anton and Mike sit on the couch watching.

'This, this, this one? One, one, one of these?' says Tim.'

'Might fit Marie?' says Mike.

Tim throws it onto a pile.

'This one, this one?'

'Phoebe.'

'This, this, this, this?'

'Nah.'

It goes on for a while. Anything that one of their friends can use goes onto one pile while everything else gets flung onto another.

That is, until Mike says no to a cotton dress. Tim doesn't throw it onto the rejects pile but just stands there.

'Come on, we haven't got all day,' says Mike.

Tim grips the dress.

'Tui,' he says.

One word. Short. Clipped.

Mike groans.

'No, Tim. Tui wouldn't want that shit. Have you ever even seen her wear a dress?'

Anton looks on, bemused. He tries to imagine Tui wearing it, but can't. It's an old-fashioned blue and white cotton dress. Feminine, casual, pretty, and nothing like what he's seen Tui wear. She's tough. Actually, all the young women in the valley seem tough to Anton, but she's really tough. He hasn't seen her in anything other than cargo shorts, combat boots, big woolly jumpers, and camo. But Tim looks so fragile Anton doesn't want to be discouraging.

'Why don't you give it to her and see?' says Anton.

Mike turns to face Anton.

'Do you *want* him to have the crap kicked out of him?'

'She wouldn't do that! Surely?'

'You don't know her very well, do you?' he says to Anton before turning to Tim. 'She doesn't want pretty shit; she wants knives and grub. She's the angriest bitch I know.'

'Angry, angry, angry, yes,' says Tim quietly, 'Because she's got nothing pretty, nothing nothing nothing pretty nothing pretty.'

Tim looks scared but defiant, like he knows he's about to get a hiding but is refusing to run away.

'Your funeral,' says Mike as he gets up and heads inside. 'I'll find a bag.'

Mike walks down the hall towards the back of the house. He steps into the kitchen and where the back door should be there's a clear view of the garden. The western wall's lying flat on the lawn like a badly built deck.

Anton comes up behind him and notes the sun heading for the hills.

'Time to go perhaps? It'll be dark soon,' he says.

'Yeah, hang on.' Mike rummages through the kitchen cupboards. 'Here we go.' Mike pulls out half a dozen supermarket bags. He holds up one with a faded New World logo on it for Anton. On the other side of the wall there are still cupboards and Mike pulls out some cans of food and puts them in a bag.

Anton opens the drawers.

'How did this house escape the tsunami?' he says. 'It's a miracle.'

Mike laughs.

'How high's the wave now? What are they saying?'

Anton pauses.

'Um, it was twenty metres, wasn't it?' Anton falters when Mike remains silent. 'Was it higher? I've also heard thirty and well—'

'Twenty metres? Thirty metres?' Mike pulls a face. 'I almost would've liked to have seen that.' He stuffs the spare bags inside the one with cans.

'It wasn't twenty metres …?' says Anton.

'Don't be a dick. It was one. Two, tops. The real problem was the land tilted, sinking in the west and rising in the east, leaving some of it under water level, then the wave on top of that. This side was already elevated, got lifted a bit more, and it's away from the river and foreshore. The liquefaction and houses falling off their piles did more damage. Across the harbour the sinking was more dramatic, as you saw. But that affected businesses more than homes. There's plenty of houses like this with no water damage. People just don't want to come over here. It's not the tsunamis you have to watch out for though, it's the bulldozers and developers and the government seizing supposedly uninhabitable buildings. Here, hold this.'

Mike passes him the bags and climbs up on the bench to get into the very top cupboards.

'I thought we were just after an 'offering'?' says Anton.

'Yeah, but we're here, aren't we? Hey look, Chicken Tonight,' says Mike as he holds up a glass jar of sauce as though it's a trophy.

*

'Nothing lasts forever ...' Pete pauses, as if thinking of what to say next. He hums a little, then continues speaking in a slow monotone. He talks about holding candles in the rain, in November of all months.

That's the second time he's mentioned cold November rain, thinks Anton. Is it significant? It does rain a lot here. Some sort of microclimate thing going on perhaps, or maybe just bad luck. Anton starts to wonder if it's perhaps a metaphor. Pete continues talking … about more rain. Perhaps living in the bush has made him obsess about the weather?

Anton sits silently waiting for more until Mike elbows him in the ribs and stage whispers, 'He wants you to ask your question.'

Anton isn't sure what he's supposed to say. Mike and Tim seem to think he has a burning question that needs answering but he all he wants is to be left alone to collect some data, analyse it, and then go home. No more festivals or quests or anything.

'Everybody needs some time on their own, don't you?' says Pete looking directly at Anton for the first time.

Well, that's weird. Even the kererū sitting on a low branch directly outside the crude window of the shack stops preening and cocks her head to the side. It's as though Pete is answering the thoughts in Anton's head.

'Um, yeah,' stammers Anton. 'I do need some time alone actually.'

'Sometimes I need some time on my own,' says Pete, which is odd since he appears to live on his own and there's no one around for miles. Everyone else is crammed into houses, the marae, the squash club, the rugby league club. As though huddled together they might be safer. But Pete's shack is half a day's walk down the valley.

'Sometimes I need some … Everybody needs some … Don't you know you need some?'

Anton finds himself nodding, along with Mike and Tim.

Pete sighs, resumes smoking an old wooden pipe, and gazes into the distance. The kererū shuffles then steps off the branch and almost hits the ground before rising with the heavy slow beats of wings that sound like the whop whop of a helicopter in slow motion. She rises and lands in a tree only metres away.

Mike crawls forward, quietly, reverently, and places a can of Tui beer on a plank that serves as a coffee table. Pete gives the slightest of nods and the visitors quietly rise and leave.

Walking down the track Anton thinks of all the valuable research time that's being lost in yet other senseless journey, when Mike clears his throat.

'Pete says you can go off by yourself tomorrow to look for your birds.'

Anton stops walking. 'He did?'

Tim stares at his feet looking unhappy. Mike punches him in the arm.

'Yeah. There's a Community Board meeting tomorrow at midday, just pop along to that so it can get signed off and you're good to go. You go look for your birds, eh?'

He turns and keeps walking.

Anton stands on the path looking at their backs as they vanish around a bend, and he looks back at the hut on the hill. Just a moment ago he thought it was all a waste of time, but somehow Pete has given him the freedom he wants so badly.

*

The Community Board meeting is at the Flying Jug. It's packed. There are certainly more people living in the valley than Anton had imagined. Where are they all living? Surely not in the broken houses? Are they living in cars? In tents? In the bush? Then again, he's heard there were increasing numbers of people living in the bush all through the country before the earthquake, so why not after it, too?

Everyone in the pub seems to know each other, and Anton feels very conspicuous. He overhears two elderly women whispering loudly,

'That's the university man, that is. The one studying birds.'

'What for?'

'What's that?'

'I said, what for? What's he studying birds for? That won't get him a job now, will it?'

Anton moves along. He sees Henry and Derek on a makeshift stage with a lot of other people he hasn't yet met or been introduced to.

'I call this meeting to order!' shouts Henry.

The crowd erupts in catcalls, hoots, and various people shouting orders.

'Order of chips!'

'Order of beer!'

'ORDER!' Henry thumps a builder's mallet on a chopping board over and over again. 'I will not have insolence in the house!'

'It's not a house, it's a tavern!'

'It's not a pub, it's a jug!'

'A flying jug!'

Henry pummels the makeshift gavel on the board until all the smart arses give up and turn to talk to their mates instead. As the room settles down, Anton remains near the bar. He's about to take a seat when one of the retired folks smacks him in the back of his knees with a stick and tells him to get out of it. Which, he decides, is for the better as he can escape if the meeting has no useful information for him. He's been to enough meetings in his life to know they're mostly full of bureaucratic busybodies with a sense of self-importance. It's time to stop talking about birds and start observing, conserving, catching, banding, hatching, handling, writing down numbers in neat little columns in a notebook. He wants to be alone in the bush with the birds.

No, that's not true. Anton feels that he should get on, start with his research, do what he's paid to do. But he can't summon any actual enthusiasm.

Henry starts shouting over the hubbub and the crowd settle down.

'I hereby call this meeting to order. On the agenda is the renaming of streets, the conserving of water, and the concessions to Anton's bird antics.'

'Bird antics?' Anton can't help but say out loud.

'Order! Order! Members of the public are reminded that unless they have registered to speak in advance they are here as observers only and do not have speaking rights.'

'But you're having a meeting about me?'

'Order! Order! You are on your last warning.' Henry holds the mallet by the head and points the handle at Anton. 'You will be removed forthwith if you so much as make a peep from hereon in. Do you understand?'

Anton's not sure if an answer of *yes* will be considered a *peep* so merely nods. He sees Mike leaning against the wall laughing quietly, before giving a slight nod in what could perhaps be interpreted in a reassuring way, or perhaps in a *fuck he's a useless sod* kind of way. Anton's heartbeat hammers loudly in his ears.

The meeting resumes.

Derek Hope reads a long and nonsensical bureaucratic memo over rules and regulations in the valley which Anton can't see a point to, a long dreary discussion on changing the spelling of street names to reflect their pronunciation in the local dialect, before the chairperson says the topic for the *Conversation about Conservation* session today is *pesky birds*. He says *pesky* as though it's a technical term.

Anton's not quite sure what's going on.

'You've all had sufficient time to consider the proposal,' says Henry, 'So let's vote. All in favour of removing pesky birds in line with DOC proviso 172 say aye.'

'Aye.' A monotone chorus of voices call out.

'All who do not want to support their community in this worthwhile and honourable initiative say nay.'

No one says anything. Anton's tempted to say nay just to make a point, even though he clearly does not have voting rights, but he's not entirely sure what they're voting for.

The mallet is employed once more, as though an auction has taken place and Anton's the lucky bidder.

'The motion has passed unanimously. 'Congratulations Dr Anton!'

The hall erupts in applause. Old ladies turn around, smile, and say, 'Didn't we do well?'

Young men with serious faces stand, thump each other on the back, and say things like, 'Right, let's get started then. No point hanging around here.'

Anton sees Mike gesturing with a nod to the door, indicating that it's time to leave. He sidesteps the people with beaming smiles trying to shake his hand on the way out.

'What the hell was all that about?'

'They've banned the pesky birds from the valley.'

'Pesky birds?'

'Any that aren't native.'

'What? Why?'

'Something to do with trying to undo all the damage people have done. Last week they voted to cut down all the old pōhutukawa on Main Street because they're not native.'

'I thought pōhutukawa *were* native?'

'Yeah, nah, well they are, but not to here, they're not. The natural southern boundary of those trees is sixty km north of here, so they cut them all down. And now it's the same with the birds. So, all of them are on the way out.' Mike sweeps a hand signalling the swallows swooping over the lawn and around the flowerbeds.

'But they're native.'

'No, they aren't. They weren't here before we got here.'

'Well, no, I believe they came here in a storm in 1958, but that still technically counts as native as long as people didn't introduce them. They're just not endemic, that is, not unique to here.'

'Right. Well, I don't know. They're still immigrants, right? They might get all caught up in this.'

'How can anyone realistically do that? Put up signs and tell them to leave? Why would anyone even try to do that?'

'Are you hungry?'

'Hungry? Um, yeah, I suppose.'

'There you go then. Introduced birds are now on the menu. We need to feed everyone somehow, and it fits in with their view of the world that those birds should never have come here. The town wants to help you. They think it'll help the native birds if there are no others around.'

Anton lets out a groan.

'That's not how it works. Any technique they use for killing birds is bound to affect the natives too.

Look, I don't understand why on earth you didn't vote against it?'

Mike shuffles his feet. Looks down. Quiet voice.

'I don't have voting rights.'

'Why ever not?'

Mike takes a long time to answer.

'There were forms that needed filling in …'

Both of them remain quiet for a while. Anton remembers something.

'Hey, I thought the whole valley is supposed to become vegetarian?'

'Supposedly. I'm not supposed to kill deer, pigs, and goats to feed people even though they destroy the vegetation the native birds rely on, but people are now allowed to eat blackbirds, sparrows, and starlings. Look, I don't give a toss what anyone else does or doesn't want to eat, that's their choice. I just don't want to be told what I can and cannot eat by a bunch of hypocrites who think imported soymilk in foil-lined cartons is environmentally friendly and killing introduced pests is not.'

Anton and Mike walk in silence for a bit, heading up towards Kōwhai Grove.

'Have you seen Tim?' says Mike.

'No. Come to think of it. Why?'

'Because he needs to protect Starlight.'

'No one would hurt Starlight, would they?'

'That new declaration means introduced birds are now going to be eradicated, killed, shot, trapped, eaten. There are no exceptions. Starlight's going to end up in bird pie. We need to let Tim know.'

'I was planning on heading up to the ridge to check for—'

'No, he won't be up there. Go up to the east.'

'I'm sorry but I need to—'

'You need to help find Tim.'

'Look, I've seen the way this valley does things. If it's anything like the way they catch cats, not a single bird is at risk. And I have work to do.'

'Yeah, look, I know they're mostly all talk, which is why we ignore them and do our own thing. But that festival was more … symbolic, if you like. They wanted to make you feel welcomed. But this is different. There's talk of poisoning Mrs Henderson's bird bath, smearing glue on the phoenix palm. That sort of thing. Even if they don't kill anything Tim will be upset. Can you just help me find him?'

'You really care about him, don't you?'

'Yeah, of course I do. You know that flat, next door to Marie's? Me, Ava, Tui, Jay, and Tim all grew up there. Mr and Mrs Grey took us all in, others too, though we're the only ones left. A whole house of misfits.'

'I don't think I've met Mr and Mrs Grey, have I?'

Mike gives a weak smile. 'You did actually. Remember that building that pancaked opposite the place we stayed in town? That's where they were working the night of the earthquake, cleaning offices. That's their tomb.'

'Oh, I am so sorry, I've been insensitive.'

'It's alright. You weren't to know. But thing is, they worked morning, noon, and night to raise other people's kids, kids no one else wanted, and they never wanted anything for themselves. And they looked after Tim when no one else would.'

Anton nods sympathetically.

'And they're not here to look after him anymore, but we are. I do it for them as much as for Tim. So, are you going to give me a hand or not?'

Anton looks up at the hills, green in the foreground, blue and misty in the distance.

'Of course, it'll be my pleasure to help.'

'Good. You head southeast. I'll organise the others to look too, and we'll all meet at the golden Ford Fiesta at dusk. I'll bring food. Just find Tim.'

Tim once read a book about Mozart's starling. Mozart bought the bird off a guy because it had learned the opening from *Piano Concerto no. 17 in G* and sang it perfectly. Starlings are amazing mimics. They can easily imitate other birds, dogs, people, washing machines. But this story was not so well known in the valley because starlings are pests. Not native. Not endemic. Therefore, they have no redeeming qualities.

Anton's not native, but he does have redeeming qualities. Although when he arrived in the country people at the university began asking him about colonisation and linguistic imperialism, and if he ever complained about anything they told him he could fuck off back to where he came from, but he can sing. Surprisingly, for someone who when talking can stumble, stutter even, when nervous. But he can sing with a quality of sound Tim hasn't really heard much, the sound of adoration. Tim's heard drunken yelling, committee shouting, rugby cheering. But not a lot of singing, and not this quality of singing. A sound in his head but not in his bones. For him singing has always been birds.

When Dicky travelled from Yorkshire to Awaawa all those decades ago he was glad to hear the songs of home here, the beautiful songbirds, the blackbirds, the starlings, the thrushes. The birds he knew so well were already here waiting for him, the chaffinches, greenfinches, goldfinches, redpolls welcomed him his first morning. His wife Annette, a local lass, hated them though. For years. 'They're not native,' she'd mutter, almost spitting, shooing them away from the back lawn where Dicky scattered breadcrumbs. It was only after she was quite vocal, almost rude, expressing her distaste towards the birds on an extended trip back to Bempton Cliffs one time that Dicky pointed out that those birds *were* native over there in merry old England. There had been an awkward silence but afterwards Annette had secretly started to listen to their singing with a slightly more charitable ear.

Tim's starling was raised from a chick when the tree it was in got chopped down by the council so the land under the trees could be used as fill for a new bike path. Tim saw the nest fall. Quickly, especially for a bumbling uncoordinated kind of guy, he leapt forward and scooped it up mid-air and took it home.

Well, took it to a patch of bush with a tarp and a packing crate he sometimes used, where he found a new spot in a tree to put the nest. He ran down to Colin Mitchell's Chemist and asked the pharmacist for a syringe. The pharmacist had been well trained in spotting drug seeking behaviour and was firm in his refusal, even after Tim explained in detail and with much anxiety about the baby bird. Mrs Henderson, waiting with a prescription for Mr Henderson in her hand, said, 'Give him the damned syringe, I haven't got all day to wait around at my age. It's Timothy for pity's sake. He's the most harmless creature around.'

Tim thought she was referring to the starling as being the harmless creature, thankfully. And so, it was with a syringe that Tim fed a baby starling and talked to it every day in a way that no one had ever talked to Timothy. Goodness knows where he learned to be such a conversationalist.

Tui told Tim about how her great-grandmother used to get tūī to sing karakia, to greet guests when they arrived, or warn when enemies approached. She thought Tim could do the same with the starling. Get it to tell them if the government inspectors were coming, or the absentee landlords, or the police. Or even get it to sing something to make everyone laugh, cheer them up a bit, take their minds off of mere survival.

But Tim didn't like the idea of that. Of teaching a bird human language when what Tim wanted was to learn bird language. He thought of the starling as a friend, an equal, a family member. He didn't want to teach the starling to talk as a trick, to impress people, or freak them out. Maybe he talked to the starling because the starling was like him, abandoned and alone in the world. Tim talked to the starling because there was no one else who would listen to Tim talk, and no one else who would talk to a bird.

But a bird living in a flat picks up on an awful lot of language, and an awful lot of song.

There are parallel universes where we have all fallen out of trees at some stage and Tim has picked us up and placed us back in our nests. We all need that sometimes. For someone to scoop us out of the air, pop us in a nest, say soothing words. We've all been tiny chicks at some stage, bald and unable to fly, on the brink of falling.

There's a long history of eating birds, birds that are not chickens or ducks or geese. Four and twenty blackbirds were baked in a pie once upon a time. Kererū would be better, one or two birds for the same amount of meat as two dozen thrushes, but that's still frowned upon by some.

It's now open season on the introduced species, the ones who *should never have been here in the first place.*

But that includes Starlight, and that's problematic because we all quite like Starlight. He's hilarious when bathing in Mr Henderson's birdbath singing *Rain* by Dragon.

So, let's all put down our gardening tools, our hammers, our cake batter, our DIY books, our clipboards. Let's go look for some damned silly bird and the man who loves him. Let's see what they're up to and if they can be saved, just this once, from some hurt in their lives.

*

The ridge to the south's always a good bet. It's longer than walking along the streets as the crow flies but avoids encounters with elderly homeowners looking for nice young men to chat to. It avoids passing the council-erected notices saying building condemned, occupation forbidden. It avoids the crumped houses and the crushed spirits. Anton doesn't have to pass cars that look abandoned during the day, but which have been carefully sealed up to keep warm at night to be used as extra bedrooms. The hot water bottles tucked under the seats will later be filled by those indoors. If he walks along the southern ridge there's no one heading out of the valley, looking to escape or for *offerings* or *findings*, or further inland to look for pigs or deer. The trees aren't as tall so it's not so interesting for bird life, but Anton is able to sit on the ridge and from there he spots Mr Henderson popping out to the letterbox, as he does each morning, despite postal services having stopped ages ago. Looking for the insurance letter that never arrives.

Mr Henderson carries a broom and at first Anton thinks he's sweeping cobwebs from the trees, the carport, the trellis. He appears to be dancing around the lawn and Anton quickly realises that the old man is in fact scaring away the sparrows who up until yesterday he'd fed daily on the lawn. Instead of dropping bread he's pacing back and forth as the birds fly from one side of the garden to the other, waiting for their food to be scattered. Anton looks frantically at other houses, other streets. He sees Derek and Susan carrying a badminton net, Ryan with a whip moving from tree to tree, Jessica blowing a whistle. Clouds of birds swoop up in one spot and down again in another. Anton can hear the alarm calls all over the valley, the calls of the birds, the calls of the people.

It has begun.

He had been heading up the hill to find Tim, to keep Mike happy. Now he's apprehensive. He picks up his daypack and tightens the straps. Instead of looping around, going the long way round, he descends straight down the hill back into the valley.

Anton runs down Main Street without any cable-clad slipper-shod interruptions of requests for errands or gossip or *what's your name again young man?* and up the opposite side into the bush on the eastern hills. He circles around Pine Peak to the north and back and then heads down the ridge towards the sea. The sea is a long way off of course, not even within view, nor earshot, yet. *Towards the sea* is merely a direction marker. It makes Anton a little nervous, nonetheless. He thinks about Pete surfing the wave up the valley, an idea that he's previously dismissed as local legend, especially since Mike laughed at the idea. But, walking in that direction now, alone, he decides to stay up on the ridge, judging the distance to the valley floor, wondering how far above sea level he is. Catches himself wondering. Berates himself, but mentally measures again.

And then without realising it he finds he's taken the turnoff to Pete's shack and is walking up to the door, only at the last-minute thinking, fuck, I haven't brought anything. He pauses, about to turn around, hand raised to knock but not knocking when Pete opens the door.

'Anton!'

'Pete. Hi, I appear to have come empty-handed. My apologies.'

'Nothing lasts forever.'

A reference to the scarcity of any packaged food products no doubt. Or is he referring to the tradition of bringing an offering? Pete nods at the deck made of packing cases and the two men sit down. Pete rolls a cigarette with proper cigarette papers and tobacco. Anton stares without meaning to. Pete offers it to Anton who, though he doesn't smoke, feels it rude not to take the rolly and start smoking. He coughs a little more than he wants to, but less than he should, given his lack of experience. Pete pats him on the back and takes the rolly back, carefully stubbing it out in a way that keeps the precious tobacco from falling out. He smokes his own rolly in silence and when the cigarette has burnt down to almost nothing Pete lets the wind lift the small white slip of paper into the air where it flutters around in an eddy by the door before being swept up and flying away.

Pete sighs.

'Nothing lasts forever,' he says again, looking at his empty hands. He nods several times then heads back indoors. The door closes with the sound of wood and wood slowly being squeezed together, door in doorframe, like a needy couple.

Anton stands. Feels silly for a second, not knowing what's expected of him or what, if anything, he should have said, and then just as quickly relaxes. The air in the bush ebbs and flows. The earthworms keep burrowing, the karearea keep hovering, the female cicadas sit in silence because female cicadas don't sing. Everything continues on, and so too does Anton down the ridge, listening out for Tim, for Starlight, watching the birds in the distance for any movement upwards from the canopy that might indicate movement through the undergrowth.

*

The idea of a starling as a pet is often discounted, ignored, laughed at, dismissed. A bit like Tim. But look at him now. Watch the way he blends into the bush so seamlessly that Anton walks right past him. Anton's on a mission and nothing's going to stop him!

It takes a good few minutes for Anton to stop and think, *Fuck! Was that Tim?* and turn around and head back. Tim meanwhile has roamed over the ridge into the neighbouring valley, following the trail of a deer, so it takes Anton a little time to find him again.

'Tim! I'm so glad to bump into you!'

Tim doesn't look up. He acknowledges Anton with a raised forefinger, such as you used to see as a friendly *wave* used by drivers on country roads. There being no cars left the wave has migrated in search of new habitats, hoping for a better life, new opportunities. It has found Tim and a way of acknowledging the hearing of audible language without the need to use it himself. Tim is busy peering at the leaf litter.

'Can you see the kōkako wattles?' says Tim.

Anton sees nothing but doesn't really look, not really.

'It's unlikely there are any kōkako here. It's a bit far south to be honest.'

'There.' Tim points at the ground.

Anton continues to look at Tim. 'Kōkako like to sit higher up in the canopy, in tawa trees …'

Tim turns his head slightly while still looking down. 'Werewere kōkako, kōkako wattles. *Look*!'

Anton looks where Tim's pointing and sees brilliant blue fungi, like something from a kid's book rather than the muted colours of the bush. 'Oh, I've never seen them before.'

'Yes, you have.'

'I assure you, I haven't.'

'Notice dollar fifty, fifty-dollar note.'

Anton thinks Tim's offering him a bet and is just

about to decline when Tim continues.

'One man, one building.' Tim mimes turning something over. 'One bird, one fungus. One fifty dollar.'

'Oh.' Anton reaches into his pocket to get his wallet before remembering he doesn't carry money anymore. 'That's interesting. You don't often see fungi on bank notes, nor insects, nor any invertebrates for that matter.'

Tim turns his head and looks at Anton, encouraging him to continue, to *rabbit-on*, as Anton's mother would say. So, he obliges.

'Did you know that a whopping ninety seven percent of animals are actually invertebrates? Most things are spineless!' He laughs at his own joke. 'Not many people know that.'

'Why?' says Tim.

'Sorry?'

'Why no one knows? No one knows why?'

'Well, there's not much interest to be honest. It's easy to get grants for mammals, mammals and birds, but creepy crawlies aren't cute. So, not enough research gets done. There's no momentum.'

'You like bugs, butterflies. Butterflies bug you.'

'I do, yes. But it wasn't meant to be, evidently.'

Tim leans in close and looks directly at Anton. 'Anton likes ants. Anton's like ants. Ants like Anton. Anton, ants. Ants Anton. Ant. You're Ant, not Anton.'

Anton laughs. 'Is that my new nickname?'

'No.' Tim peers closely. 'It's your destiny.'

Anton suddenly remembers why he needed to find Tim but he's unsure what to do with him. Tell him about the town meeting? Warn him about the threat to Starlight? Or just get him to Mike? 'Is Starlight with you?'

'Starlight is stars right? Starlight, light from stars. No starlight when sun lights the sky. There's sunlight so no starlight. Come back tonight.' Tim still looks intently at the fungi, carefully moving aside a single fallen leaf with a twig to get a better view.

'No,' says Anton. 'Starlight, the bird, the starling. Is Starlight here?'

Tim pauses, looks up. 'No.' Brows knitted.

'I think you might need to keep him away from the houses, at least for a while. It's not, well that is to say, it's not entirely safe.'

Where's a safe place for the wind? Where would you tell the wind to go? What would threaten the wind? It's no more use asking the wind where it would take refuge than asking a tree in which direction it wants to grow. The answer's absent or meaningless or merely words words words or sounds without meaning.

What's the sound Tim's making? Is it grief or rage or fear? Are we surprised that someone so meek, so quiet can make such a sound like a massive branch breaking above our heads? Or is it the sound of a vacuum being filled, a whoosh of air into a space where there was none before? A feeling of the barometer falling rather than a sound, perhaps? It's an aircraft door being sucked out mid-flight. A shock wave that hits before it's heard and the shrapnel slices through.

Anton saw a teacher yelling at a kid at a train station once. Except she was yelling with no sound at all, as she was using sign language. The hands flew so fast they were a blur and no one outside the group knew what was being said, not literally, but everyone knew. Everyone on the platform was silent and slowly edged away, embarrassed.

The sound of Tim moving through the bush is noisy as hell and yet no sound at all. Tim is the roar of a waterfall, the wind in the beech forest. Every creature that makes a noise in the forest fills a frequency niche. Tim fills all the frequencies left vacant by extinct species, fills them all at once. It's a haunting sound. The wind takes every sound and shifts it somewhere else.

Is Tim rushing down towards town to fight with the community leaders, or is he running up and over the hills away from the town, or is he crouching under a fallen tree trunk hiding, thinking, *What to do? What to do?* Or is he doing all three things at once and an onlooker – Anton, say – doesn't know what to do or think and worries he's witnessing some kind of fit.

Finally, the wind abates, the sound in the beech trees drops from a wailing to an empathetic rustling, the cicadas stop screaming but continue calling, the birds, oh the birds, they're still squawking, stopped flapping, flying, fuming over the whole affair. Anton squats, lays a hand on Tim's shoulder as gently as a leaf falling from a tree.

'Mike said he and I are to meet at the golden Ford Fiesta. Do you want to come too, or should I leave you here? And let Mike know where you are?'

I shouldn't have told him, thinks Anton. I should've left that to Mike. I've no idea what I'm doing here or why, or why I care about a starling. It's only a starling after all, not … and Anton was going to finish that thought with kākāriki or kererū or kiwi or some kind of bird but he can't think of a bird that had more right, or less, than Starlight to live here.

Tim sits in the undergrowth, not moving, then starts whistling quietly the notes to *Bohemian Rhapsody*. Anton realises that he's heard fragments of the same tune from the tūī that frequents the flax in Mr Henderson's garden, and korimako in the bush behind too. The bogans taught the starling, the starling taught the tūī, the tūī taught the korimako.

And around it goes. Extract the sounds, the pure sounds that belong in the valley. And what would they be?

The kākā are coming back. What does a kākā sound like? Like Aucklanders wolf-whistling. Now all the kākā in Wellington have a whistle that locals love, *The wild natural sounds of the kākā!* they enthuse. Except they're not natural kākā sounds at all, but the half-remembered, half-rendered sounds of an Auckland ranger. Are the sounds made by Woof Woof, the tūī at the sanctuary, unnatural because he says, *Come up here, look at the kākāriki*, but the sounds of him mimicking the korimako are natural? What if he mimics a song thrush? Any more or any less natural? What about the tūī on Kōwhai Grove who used to mimic cell phone ringtones, tones that Mike recorded for Tim so he could use the mimicking call as his ringtone? And when Tim moved into Marie's sleepout the starling mimicked the phone's recording of the tūī mimicking a cell phone. How about the tūī kept in cages by Tui's ancestors who sang karakia? Are native birds singing native songs more natural sounding than those mimicking Freddie Mercury or David Bowie?

The sounds of car engines have been tweaked so they sound like large mammals roaring. Engines that sound like roaring lions are preferred over those that sound like Tasmanian devils or rats. The engines of the cars on the streets of Awaawa no longer roar or squeak or speak.

*

Mike's sitting on the bonnet of the golden Ford Fiesta. Golden is a bit of a stretch. It's more yellow, much to the regret of the former owner when it came back from the panel beaters after a crash. (*You said it would be golden!* he'd yelled. The spray painter had taken off his cap, scratched his head, and said, *Yeah well, it said golden-yellow in the catalogue. What can you do?*)

Mike has his thumbs hooked in the belt loops of his black jeans, leg bent and foot resting on the bumper, watching Anton and Tim approach. Cars may be going literally nowhere, but they still provide an air of sophistication, of coolness-rating, of don't-worry-we-aren't-beaten-just-yet. Mike knows instinctively how to pose in a way that instils confidence in onlookers. Anton relaxes a little and the kāhu on the powerline decides to resume searching the paddocks for lunch.

Mike begins drumming his fingers. Not through impatience, mind you, but without thinking. He was a great drummer back in the day, but with no electricity and therefore no electric guitars there's just not the motivation for others to play anymore, and he's never liked playing alone. He's moving his fingers unconsciously, the way crickets or frogs or ocean waves or leaves dripping with rain make sound.

'You hungry Tim?'

Tim, arms wrapped around himself, shakes his head.

'You've got to eat Tim.'

'You said, you said no, nobody, nobody, nobody. Nobody would hurt the birds.'

'We'll find Starlight, he'll be alright.'

'The birds. Birds birds.' Tim speaks slowly, stressing the 's' sound at the end. It sounds like when you walked past the bamboo in Fung's garden and all the pesky birds with husky voices say, *hi. Hi, hi*. For a second Anton wonders if Tim's stressing the plural form or mimicking the birds.

Anton hadn't thought of the other birds, only Starlight, and the look on Mike's face shows that neither had he.

Mike shrugs. 'I'm sorry mate, but people've got to eat. All those cows shitting in Hill Valley means there's nothing to fish for in the river anymore. And not many bastards are mad enough to go out in the harbour.'

Tim says nothing. Mike reaches in through the Fiesta window and lifts a backpack from the front seat. He pulls out a little can of tuna, a big loaf of fresh bread, a bunch of half-wilted green leaves, and a thermos. 'Come on, I've brought us a feast.' He draws a parcel of newspaper from his shirt pocket and carefully unfolds it to reveal a choice of old lollies – a jet plane, a gumdrop, a couple of pink smokers, a caramel, and a green licorice allsort.

Tim's eyes go wide. 'Where, where, where?'

'Been saving them. Thought you might need a pick me up.'

Tim nods slightly. He shuffles forward and examines the lollies in Mike's hand. He takes his time making up his mind and Anton can see Mike having to bite his tongue. Finally, after about a minute, Tim choses a smoker and a jet plane. Anton grabs a gumdrop and a caramel, and they all sit down to eat.

The food is the best Anton has had in a long time, but he's distracted thinking through the implications of the new food source. If all the introduced birds are being trapped or shot, then it will upset the native birds too. His data will be messed up. He'll have to stay longer, or come back later, or find a new location to collect data. He sees now why Mike made him go to the Community Meeting. It wasn't just to protect Starlight and Tim. They're all in this together.

'All we need to do,' says Mike, 'is find Starlight and keep him inside or on a leash or in a cage or with Tim at the other end of the valley.'

But Starlight's a starling and starlings love to live

in big noisy flocks. Starlight and Tim are quite different in that way. Arranged marriages can work better than *love matches* because the parents have considered the temperaments of both parties, and how well matched they are. Friendships are usually never *arranged*. Tim likes, or tolerates perhaps, small groups, one other person, or no one. Starlight likes big raucous parties, lots of drinking and eating anything that comes along and laughing loudly and joining in a big singsong, a big raucous drunken singalong. Tim likes his own company. Starlight says the more the merrier. If he were in Europe, he'd have joined a group of a million birds or more of boy racers, zooming around the sky, sending chills down the spines of the superstitious, sending chills up the spines of those watching in awe. If you haven't watched a good murmuration lately, or ever, pop yourself down in front of a screen and watch one. Or, if there's no electricity, in front of a plate glass window overlooking a likely spot, like from a house on a hillside. Or, if there are no houses, climb a tree and pop yourself down on a branch with a view. The murmurations here aren't as impressive as the ones in Europe, sure, but Starlight has great ambitions, wants to be part of something more than just the phoenix palm get-togethers in Susan's garden at dusk. Starlight dreams of bigger things.

*

Anton sits in Marie's dining room with *a nice cup of tea* warming his hands. He tried explaining that, despite being English, he doesn't like tea, doesn't usually drink it, doesn't want to use up her precious supplies, but Marie just cocks her head to one side and says something like,

'But what do you do when you just want, you know, a nice cup of tea?'

So, he sits and sips and tries not to pull a face. Marie pops her knitting on the table.

'Right-o. Let's get on with it. What's the matter, then?' she says.

'Nothing's the matter.'

'Don't give me that. You came in here with a face on you saying your knickers are in a twist about something or other.' Marie reaches across and pats his hand. 'What's bothering you dear?

Anton's emotions burst out of him like gorse seeds

popping on a hot day. He tells her all about Tim and the starling that whistles *Bohemian Rhapsody* except for the last two notes, and all about the community meeting, and how upsetting the pesky birds will upset *his* birds too and therefore his data, and how the cat festival was a monumental waste of time (she puckers her lips a little at that comment and straightens the pleats of her skirt but he's too riled up to notice), and how Mike says they need the birds to feed the people, and how people came first, and how ludicrous the idea of killing all the introduced birds to help the native ones is, and how Anton needs Tim to help him locate the kiwi and all the others, and how he's always a little hungry and is sick of packets of sugarless biscuits from the factory and wonders why can't they produce some sustaining food, and, and, and ...

Marie sighs. 'I'll put the jug on for another cuppa and we can have a little chat about what to do, shall we?'

'*And*,' says Anton, 'how I do *not* like tea, and no one listens to me!'

Marie just laughs and pats him on the arm. 'But you're English!' She hums a little tune to herself while busying with the cups and milk, teapot, and jug. A cockroach scuttles alongside her slippers and under the stove but she doesn't seem to notice.

*

Starlings are called starlings because they have white speckles, like stars, but only for some of the year. When Starlight first lost his speckles, Tim found himself missing the stars and looked up into the sky to see which constellations he could recognise. Mr Grey, when he got home from nightshift, liked to stand outside on winter evenings with a pair of binoculars, a headlamp, and a book. Tim learnt how to find south using the Pointers and the Southern Cross when still a toddler, and later how to know the time of year based on where constellations are in the sky.

But when Starlight lost his speckles and was visually lost to them in the murmuration of the valley one evening Tim looked up and mistook the Southern Cross for an injured Starlight, with one wing hurt but still carrying on. Maybe Mr Grey or maybe Sia had mentioned the story of the injured bird flying south and he'd forgotten, or maybe the constellation really does look like a wounded bird, or maybe Starlight was sick of the murmuration and was trying something new for a change and dressed up like a constellation in order to hide. But it gave Tim some hope, at least.

*

Marie likes Anton, likes having a young *edumacated* man around the house, likes the other ladies saying, *and how's your young man today?* And being a dab hand at making jams, relishes, preserved fruit, and the odd chutney, she does like having someone around to open jars, so she doesn't have to ask Henry, the crochety old bugger.

So, Marie sets out to plant a seed one evening after finding a little jar of jam to do the job. She flexes her arthritic hands and puts the lid on especially tightly, or as tightly as she can manage, before popping it in her pinny pocket, putting on a cardy, and setting out. She's got business to attend to, so pauses and pinches her cheeks, and nips at her lips with her fingertips. Oh, what she would do for a little lippy.

Starlight's in the phoenix palm, unbeknown to anyone on the street, least of all Tim or any of the others searching for him. He splices *I'll pop the jug on* seamlessly into his evening repertoire, for no one else's benefit but his own. He's delighted at seeing Marie walk along the street.

Mr Henderson mumbles a *hello* or something as she passes, and she smiles in reply. She stops at the ponga fence, smoothes down her skirt, then walks briskly up the path.

Henry has a doorbell even though the battery has long since stopped working and there's nothing else for Marie to do but knock on the door. Her hands are still hurting from the jam jar lid, though, so she smacks the glass jar against the door instead.

'What the devil are you up to?' Henry cries out, as he comes around the corner of the house with a watering can and sees what she's doing. 'You'll chip the paint!' He inspects the door before rounding on the intruder.

Marie smiles sweetly.

'Oh, silly me! It's my hands, they're ever so sore, look at how red they are. It's my arthritis playing up. I need a big strong bloke to open this jar for me or I'll have nothing for my tea.'

'Why doesn't that young man open it for you? What good is he if he can't open the odd jar of jam?'

'Oh,' she sighs, in her best am-dram voice. 'He's ever so upset. All the birds being shooed away are ruining all his research and he's out morning, noon, and night and there's no one around.' She passes over the rusty lidded jar.

It eventually takes Henry the use of a vice and more strength than he knew he had to open it. 'Raspberry jam, is it?' he says inspecting the contents over the top of his reading glasses.

'Raspberry? Oh, is it? Silly me. I don't like raspberry. Do you like raspberry?'

'I am a little partial as a matter of fact.'

'Oh, you have it then.' She makes eye contact and gives a quick little smile. 'Cheerio!' And she's off down the path like a shot.

'Now, look here!' Henry punches the air with the jar. 'Don't come round here knocking on my door like that again!'

Marie knocks on Henry's door morning, noon, and night for a whole week, with unopened jars, broken stools, unidentified spiders in jars – claiming to suspect them of being katipō or red-backs – instruction manuals missing vital pages, recipes with corners torn off that once held the essential ingredient, biscuit tins that bizarrely look like their lids have been hammered on.

'Woman! This has to stop!'

'Oh, I am sorry Henry,' says Marie, holding a large, framed photo of her late husband. 'I wouldn't ask but it's coming up to our anniversary and our wedding photo has somehow come off the wall. Most peculiar. I'd ask one of the young men, but they all seem to have fled up into the hills.'

Meanwhile, each morning Ryan opens Henry's gate, Jessica throws a ball onto his front lawn, and Defor gallops around the flowerbeds chasing it. When Henry inevitably thumps his fists on their door demanding they keep the mongrel on a lead Jessica politely reminds him Defor Dog's a purebred and won twenty-one races in his heyday before she goes on to bemoan the loss of the occupants of the Grey house to the bush, the dog lovers, dog patters, dog walkers, dog distractors.

Soon afterwards Komas, Manu, and Sia decide to have a sing-off, and others quickly join in. Prayers and praises, pop-songs and party-favourites are traded up and down the street, from patio to porch, from veranda to deck to front steps, one song leading immediately onto another. When the original singers start to go hoarse, Welsh, Russian, Arab, and Swiss men from throughout the valley are sought out, found, adopted, and popped onto verandas with blankets and endless cups of tea to sip and biscuits to munch while they await their turn to sing.

Henry isn't used to hearing men singing. The effect on him is somewhere between awe-inspiring and downright frightening Additionally, he can't understand half the words. All his neighbours seem to nod along, hum a tune, smile, laugh, but Henry doesn't know what it's all about. He alternates between slamming his windows closed and coming to his front steps or front gate and looking in the direction of the singing, his arms crossed, tutting loudly.

'What do you make of all of this, Arnold?' he calls over the fence.

Mr Henderson looks up from the newspaper he's reading while seated in a deckchair. 'Well, if you ask me, listening to Tim's starling singing in Evie's birdbath each morning was much more agreeable, but of course that bird is on the menu now, so I doubt we'll see him again.' He shakes the six-month-old paper and resumes reading.

Down the road Ava holds a ludicrously long ladder steady while Tui climbs up to decorate Susan's phoenix palm with Halloween streamers. Andira and Phoebe, having collected all the Diwali and Christmas lights they could find, are stringing them over shrubs, around gateposts, between white pickets, up and down the street. Fitu helps Fung thread Spring Festival lanterns through disused telephone wires hanging from the power poles while Mr and Mrs Henderson totter down their respective sides of the street knocking on doors that don't already have Hanukkah, Wiccan, or Catholic candles on windowsills and deliver some lovely beeswax ones Mr Henderson whipped up just this week.

Now *this* is a festival! A festival of festivals! The singing, the lights, the potlucks, the dancing. The generators powering the lights drone on late into the night.

'What the devil's all this?' Henry exclaims at one point, pulling Diwali lights out of his prized rose bushes. Andira mutters something about the alignment of the stars and all festivals occurring at the same time this year, before continuing past his gate at an increased speed. Henry frowns but says nothing more until next morning he finds all the local children running through his garden on an Easter egg hunt.

'I've had enough of this nonsense!' he yells, to no one in particular. 'It's *not* Easter!'

Sia leans over the fence. 'What a pity Mike's not here.' He shakes his head sadly. 'He could have paid Pete a call and seen if we'd got our dates wrong.'

An impromptu A&P show inexplicably appears on the street around lunchtime, replacing birdsong with braying, baaing, and bleating.

Henry rushes down to Derek's house and pounds on the door. 'Mr Mayor! Derek Hope! Come out here at once and look at this.'

Derek comes out and stands on his front deck polishing his glasses before perching them on his nose. 'Looks like all the farm animals are on the street, how curious!'

'I can see that. I'm not blind, man! You're the mayor, make it stop!'

'I don't see why you're so upset; you won't have to trek halfway across the valley to get the manure for your roses now.'

Marie, who just happens to be in the same neck of

the woods, pops her head over the fence.

'Morning, gentlemen! Isn't it a lovely morning?'

'Indeed, it is not!' says Henry. 'I didn't get a wink of sleep last night with all the singing, generators humming, lights blinking, and now this! Is this your doing? All this, this bleeding nonsense!'

By now Andira and Garunda, Mr and Mrs Henderson, Zara and Komas, Sia and Fitu, Ryan and Jessica, with Defor on a lead barking at all the farm animals, have congregated at the veranda of Derek's house. Even Bob and Doris have popped through the gap in the fence at the back while Daniel has joined the children running around the animals and the animals are running through the gardens, eating, or trampling the rows of white iceberg roses, the Nelly Moser clematis, federation daisies, camellias, hydrangeas, freesias, flashy dahlias, violets, and pansies.

'The kids seem to like it …' says Derek.

Henry looks down at little Jemima holding onto Derek's dressing gown with one hand while picking her nose with the other.

'There are a great many things that children enjoy,' says Henry wrinkling his nose, 'but that doesn't mean we have to follow suit! Really Des, this must stop, I don't know what has gone wrong with this street, but I will not stand for it! Do you hear me?'

'We need another meeting,' muses Derek.

A murmuration is a little like the wisdom of crowds. If you take a giant jar of jellybeans and a little notebook and write three numbers per page starting somewhere around one hundred and going up to three hundred and put a certain number of jellybeans in the jar you can run a raffle and raise a bit of cash for a school or a youth group or a sports team. People try all sort of things – counting the number of beans in a row and estimating how many columns or levels there would be in the jar, counting how many they can see. But it's always a guess in the end. All you need to do is wait until the book's almost full, add up all the guesses everyone else has made, and then divide that by the number of guesses. That will be the number or pretty damned close.

It's not the individual starling that makes a murmuration amazing, it's the group working together. It's not the individual stars we admire but the constellations or the whole Milky Way. It's not the individual person, regardless of what so many books or movies or newspapers or legends say. It's the way the community ebbs and flows, the way the heroes move along the street and the neighbours greet or ignore, shake hands or punch ribs, that forms the story. If a river has no rocks, if it has been turned into a concrete culvert, then there's no life in its stream. Rocks form eddies and calm spots where the fish hide until it's their time to swim, to spawn, to shine.

*

Anton isn't sure what another Community Board meeting can achieve but he agrees to arrive early and fill in paperwork for Mike and himself, and the other occupants of the Grey household. The forms are the most outrageously officious he's ever seen, and he's filled in a lot of paperwork in his time. It takes quite some time as he has to read all relevant rules and regulations, policies and procedures that they want permission to speak to, if the need arises. And he's being constantly interrupted by other people asking what he's doing and if he can do the same for them.

230

As soon as Henry, Derek, and the others mount the stage the meeting immediately erupts into chaos. People argue back and forth, shout others down, remind others not to shout. Henry repeatedly bangs his mallet, but it makes no difference. No one can be heard, though it doesn't stop people from talking, yelling, calling out, interjecting, nor some from stomping off only to say a few last strong words from the doorway.

At last, there's a sudden hush, a room full of turning heads. Anton looks back.

Pete has walked in.

'I thought he never came down here,' Anton whispers to Mike.

'No … he doesn't,' says Mike, looking worried.

Pete stands just inside the doors to the lobby, so most people have to twist around to face him. He says nothing. He shows no sign of being about to speak. With his shoulders hunched, he looks like a boxing bag hanging from a hook in a garage, slowly rotating. But he looks over his shoulder and motions for someone to come in. Tim, with Starlight on his shoulder, shuffles into the room and stands beside Pete, fidgeting.

'Ahh, fuck no,' says Mike putting his head in his hands.

'What's wrong?' says Anton.

'They've only gone and taught Starlight a new routine and they're about to perform it.'

'Oh! Well, it might be entertaining. Surely that's not too much of a problem, is it?'

'Put it this way,' says Mike. 'Last time they taught him to sing *The Show Must Go On* for a mate's funeral.'

'That sounds touching,' says Anton.

'Could've been,' says Mike. 'If the stupid fucker hadn't sung, *Another One Bites the Dust* instead.'

Pete clears his throat. He speaks in a halting monotone. It's hard to listen to him.

'I used to be the kind of guy…'

He speaks of smiling while crying inside, of dying. Is he suicidal? Anton can't tell.

Pete looks sideways at Tim and gives him a little nod. Tim transfers Starlight to his finger and holds him out at arm's length. A lot of people laugh, others look on curiously. Starlight starts to sing, and Tim sings too, barely audible, mumbling, and slightly out of tune. The frequency of someone frightened. But he sings. He sings of having had enough of crying, of sweating, of dying, but that he's going to spread his wings. He's going to fly!

Anton recognises it's the lyrics of an old rock song, a Bon Jovi song, sung softly, meekly, the opposite of the original.

An old lady with a hearing aid says, 'I never knew pesky birds could sing so sweetly, did you?' Others laugh and start chatting.

Mike mutters under his breath. 'Wrong tune.'

'It was only a little out of tune,' says Anton.

'Nah, wrong tune for this crowd,' he says as he stands up. He stomps on the floor twice with his steel-capped boots and claps once. Immediately the chatter dies down. Anton thinks it's an attempt to get people's attention, to quieten down the crowd. But the second time he stomps, others jump up and join in. Jay, Ava, and Tui. The third time half the room stomps and claps and the fourth time almost the whole room stomps and claps at the same time. After eight rounds, the noise is almost deafening, Mike starts singing in a deep booming voice, and it seems like the whole hall immediately joins in.

Anton recognises it instantly. An unmistakable beat. Words about boys and mud, kicking and singing, moving onto words about men and noise, blood and all manners of things he wouldn't normally relate to.

He finds himself stomping and clapping along without realising it. Singing along to *We Will Rock You* by Queen.

The sound of stomping feet and slapping hands, of singing that resembles shouting, reverberates through the ceiling and up into the sky. A starling murmuration circles overhead, swirling, singing, swarming, murmuring, the sounds falling downwards back into the room where the song suddenly stops.

The feeling in the room is electric. Absolute stillness. As though everyone's holding their breath. Anton wants to ask Mike what the words all mean but even he has the sense not the break the silence.

Henry bangs the mallet on the chopping board.

'Order! Order!'

Immediately the room explodes in complaint.

'Look I have no idea what it is that you people think you're doing, or saying for that matter, but it has to stop!' Henry's already shouting again.

Mike elbows Anton. Anton turns to him wondering why.

'I've warmed them up for you,' says Mike. 'Now

it's your turn to step up.'

Anton gulps, mind racing as he stands. He clears his throat.

Some people quieten down, out of curiosity more than anything else.

'If I could be so bold as to make an observation or two?'

'No, no, no,' says Henry. 'We will have no more nonsense.'

There's a slight twitch in Anton's left eye. He pauses, then straightens up, standing even more erect. 'With all due respect, Mr Masters, according to Article Four of the communication policy for Community Board Assemblage, under the heading Procedures, Clause Two, Paragraph One, I have the right to address the board on matters affecting my occupation and livelihood as they pertain to the agenda of this meeting, namely that the warm-blooded vertebrates constituting the class Aves not historically resident in the valley are to be extirpated by means of exposure to toxicants, via ambuscade, mucilage (natural or synthetic), bombardment, or, if not extirpated, vitiated by any aforementioned method. I therefore make peremptory request to be heard.'

Henry sits with his pen hovering above the paper, unusually having scribbled nothing down. He glances at Derek Hope who makes a face and shrugs his shoulders. 'Continue,' says Henry slowly.

All heads turn with anticipation, sensing that Anton, somehow, has the upper hand. Anton glances down at Mike who nods encouragingly.

'In order to proceed with my research, I require the ministrations of an autochthonous inhabitant with knowledge of the vernaculars of both avian and anthropoid lifeforms, as well as panoptic expertise of mycology, pteridology, ornithology, dendrology, lichenology, and botany. Upon meeting numerous local inhabitants, I have come to the conclusion that only one person in the community possesses the requisite knowledge not just of the aforementioned subjects but also expertise in local meteorology, topography, and hypsometry. That person is Timothy Grey.'

There's a combined intake of breath and everyone turns to look at Tim who's as surprised as anyone else at hearing his name spoken aloud and wonders what it all means.

'Cognisant that the cognate organisation to which

I address this prelection has interdicted introduced birds, diverting and disquieting Timothy Grey, culminating in the adjournment of the collection of data on which my journey to this location relies, I therefore move that the DOC Proviso 172 is rendered null and void in accordance with Clause Three, Paragraph Six of the Occupation and Livelihood Act, which states, and I quote—'

Henry clears his throat in such a way that stops Anton dead in his tracks. Henry slowly screws the cap on his fountain pen and puts it down precisely on the table in front of him. He looks over the top of his glasses at Anton for a long time.

'What is it, exactly,' he says, 'that you want?'

'Um, could you leave the birds alone, please?'

The crowd roars, let's assume in agreement, in encouragement, but let's also admit that it could just be because they finally understand something this very odd yet increasingly interesting young man has said. Henry half-heartedly bangs the mallet, knowing it will do no good. When the crowd finally quietens down, and a whispered conference with all the board members finishes, Henry straightens up and gives Derek a nod. Derek beams at the crowd, 'Pesky birds are off the menu.'

Anton finally has his notebook, his binoculars, his GPS, everything stuffed in a day pack and is heading down Main Street, towards the foot of the eastern hills. He's behind schedule but better late than never. He has a fairly good knowledge of most of the tracks surrounding the valley by now and has started to notice what trees are growing where and what birdlife frequents each area. He has a good feeling that kiwi will be just beyond the ridge where Pete's shack sits. Anton heads in that direction and somehow, today, for the first time he doesn't get waylaid by anyone on the road. No one waves him down, leans over their fence and asks him to run an errand or relay some gossip. Mike hasn't appeared from nowhere with some madcap quest.

After some time climbing the hills, he rounds the corner to Pete's shack and sees Pete pacing back and forth in a clearing. Like he's trying to decide whether to go into the bush or not, talking to himself, clearly upset.

'Hey, Pete.'

Pete's head snaps up. He looks agitated, scared even. He peers at Anton for a second, uncomprehending, then grins.

'All systems go,' he says, excitedly, quickly. He says something about doing your best, having a rest, something about a show. Anton can't make head or tail of it.

'It drives you fucken mad!' Pete finishes with a flourish.

'Ahh, right. Okay,' said Anton. 'I was just heading over into the next valley, actually.'

Pete's grin disappears. He frowns and starts pacing. Anton isn't sure what to do.

'You seem out of sorts,' says Anton. 'Is there something I could possibly help you with?'

Pete fidgets and doesn't look directly at Anton but down into the valley, and then back to his hut.

'What's wrong Pete?'

'We built this city … we built this city … on sausage rolls.'

'I beg your pardon?'

Pete looks like he's going to cry. He sinks down to the ground and just stares out into the valley.

Anton's about to speak again when he hears whistling and turns to see Mike coming up the track swinging a kete. Mike raises his eyebrows first in surprise and then in greeting but replaces the look with a frown when he sees Pete.

Anton walks down the track and speaks quietly. 'Something's wrong, I can't quite figure out—'

'It's alright. I got it,' says Mike, not breaking his stride, his hand patting Anton's shoulder on the way past. He approaches quietly, almost reverently crouching in front of Pete. He pushes the kete forward then moves back, sitting on the wet grass.

'I was wondering,' says Mike, 'if you had any thoughts about all of this?' He gestures vaguely at everything in the valley.

Pete sniffs, unfurls from the ball he made of his body. He sits up straight, wipes his nose on his sleeve, and slaps his own face with both palms several times before exhaling audibly.

'It's hard for me to say the things I want to say sometimes,' he begins, his voice wavering a bit.

Mike nods without making eye contact. Pete coughs and continues. He gives the longest monologue Anton has ever heard from him, in a singsong voice, half mumbling, half speaking, at times humming. He repeats the same phrases over and over. There's a lot of rhyme in his words but no rhythm, as he speaks monotonously without pause or intonation.

'Thank you for loving me,' he sniffs and wipes the tears and snot again from his face with one hand. 'Thank you for loving me,' he says again as he looks down and picks up the kete. He holds it close to his chest, his eyes closed for a moment, before opening them and staring out into the valley again.

Pete nods, stands, and says, 'You give me wings.'

He turns and walks back to his hut and quietly closes the door.

'What on earth was all that about?' says Anton.

Mike picks a dry piece of grass to chew on. 'Poor bastard was hungry. What with all the drama about Starlight I forgot to send someone up with food,' says Mike.

'Oh! I could have given him something,' says Anton indicating his pack. 'He should have said.'

'Yeah, well, it's hard to find the words to say you're hungry.'

'He did say something about sausage rolls …'

'Did he?' Mike pulls out his tobacco and starts

making a rolly with a look of concentration on his face. 'Ahh,' he laughs after a moment. 'Was it Starship?'

'Sorry, what?'

'Was it the Starship song? Did he say, *We built this city on sausage rolls?*'

'Yes, something along those lines. How did you know?'

Mike laughs. 'He always did get that line wrong. Didn't matter how much we fucken told him it was *rock 'n' roll* he always sang *sausage rolls*. Him and Tui had a punch up over it when we were at school, silly buggers.'

'Pete hit Tui? That's shocking!'

'Don't be a dick, *she* bashed *him*. Gave him a hell of a blackeye.' Mike licks the paper and lights up. 'You here for your birds?'

'Yes, I was just heading over to the next valley. Thought there might be kiwi there.'

'If you're heading this way regularly, could you drop in Pete's food?'

'Certainly.'

'Just make sure you ask him for some advice on something. Try to make it meaningful, something he has to work for. Laws of reciprocity and all that.'

'I don't always understand what he's talking about.'

'I've got some old mixtapes that might help.' Mike stands up. 'Come on, I'll walk you.'

They continue up the track together till they get to the ridge and Anton can see the ranges before him, ridges and valleys full of bush and birds and bugs and not a person nor house to be seen.

Mike rests his hand on Anton's shoulder. 'Are you meeting Tim up here?'

'No, I hadn't planned on it.'

'You'll break his heart if you don't take him along. You know that, right?'

Anton sighed.

'You've got to stop thinking of him as an assistant and give him some responsibility. Anyway, Tim told me you like bugs. Is that right?'

'Yes, I'm afraid so. To my great shame.'

Mike laughs. 'You do know, don't you, that there are giant wētā on Matiu Island?'

'I didn't, no.'

'Well, if you could stomach it again, we could stop off on the way to the city for a night. If it's giant creepy crawlies you're into there are carnivorous giant snails right here in this valley. There're giant pill millipedes, and ngāokeoke, the blue velvet worms, not giant but quite beautiful things. Just ask Tim to show you where they are.'

Anton tries to push down the excited feeling that starts bubbling up. He needs to stay focused. Just get through this. 'To be perfectly honest, I don't really have time.'

'Let me get this right,' says Mike. 'You like bugs, but birds will give you the dough you need, yeah?'

'Well, in a manner of speaking, yes.'

'And Tim loves birds. So, take him along, teach him what to do, and get him to collect some of your data while you go looking for bugs.'

'I couldn't possibly do that.'

'Why the hell not? It's something he's good at, he could probably teach you a thing or two even with all your book learning. And it would make all his faffing around in the bush count for something. We've all got to have a purpose and to contribute, and this is likely the only thing Tim *can* do. Don't take that away from him. You'd get to look for bugs. Derek gets his bird data for his eco-tourism idea. We can use your grant money for some supplies. I don't know about you, but

I'm fed up with baking soda for toothpaste. The university gets their research. You can help me with shipments. Tim gets to talk to birds. Everyone's happy.'

'Oh, I don't know, I couldn't exploit Tim.'

'Are you kidding? He'd *love* it. Anyway, ask him yourself,' Mike says pointing with his chin into the bush.

Let's all watch, shall we, as Tim makes his way up the overgrown ridge track coming from the coast. He has found a bottle of Speights and instead of saving it up until he has a question, like Mike would do, or drinking it, like Darren would do, he's bringing it straight to Pete. He clambers along the track whistling the last notes of *Bohemian Rhapsody* trying to teach an indifferent starling sitting on his shoulder how to finish what it started.

Birds don't call out in alarm as Tim moves through the bush, don't make a feathered Mexican wave, rising and falling to give away his location. As we all know, on the valley floor the ability to enter a room, a party or a town meeting say, and have no one notice your entrance nor remember you were even there, is not admired. It is, if anything, a badge of great shame.

Most won't see it as a skill, but Anton watches and recognises this skill, and he sees Tim as if for the first time. And just as Anton recognises this we turn and notice it too. We all watch.

Wasps fly out from their holes in the clay. Carnivorous snails suck up earthworms. Kōkako wattles press up through the soil. Skinks scuttle amongst the leaves. Towering kahikatea stand overlooking the valley, moving nutrients along their roots towards the seedlings still in the shade.

The earth shakes slightly.

But no birds take flight. They just readjust their footing on the branches, flutter their wings a bit, rebalance, and settle back down.

Just another readjustment of the crust of the earth. Nothing to worry about. It's just the western ranges, like a child leaving home, moving away, moving on.

A kererū perching in a rimu close by tilts her head to the side and watches Anton. Watches as Anton shifts his weight slightly, unconsciously. Anton stands on the hill and watches the world.

Also published by Piwaiwaka Press
www.piwaiwakapress.org

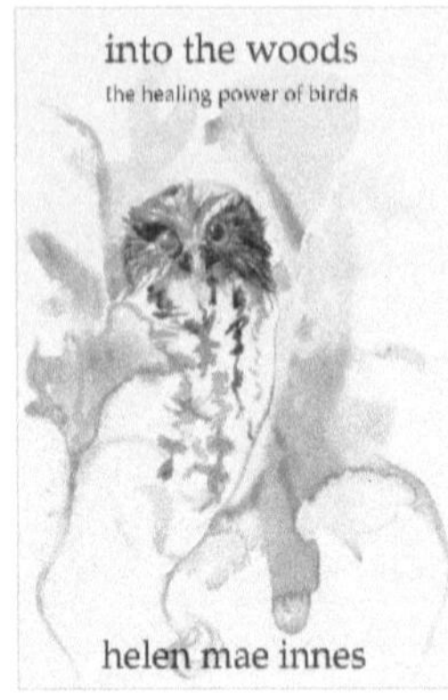

Into the Woods: The healing power of birds

Helen Mae Innes

ISBN: 978-0-473-67044-3

102 x152mm (4 x 6 in)

Page count: 80

A funny, painful, powerful story about the strange ways grief moves through us. Helen's path of recovery, from a bed she doesn't want to leave towards a natural world she doesn't know, is full of recognisable difficulties and unlikely connections. This frank and bracing little book has a bass note of personal tragedy but a top note of surprising joy.
Damien Wilkins

It happened during the spring when the kākā had first appeared in the valley. I noticed a grey warbler fledgling outside my window who couldn't get the tune quite right. He'd start singing, get a note wrong and falter, then try tentatively again. Like a child learning the recorder, I thought … like a child.

Oracles & Miracles & Zombies

Stevan Eldred-Grigg & Helen Mae Innes

ISBN: 978-0-473-66272-1

127 x 203mm (5 x 8 in)

Page count: 328

Stevan Eldred-Grigg's best-selling, award-winning novel is back – with zombies!

Little has been written about how the biters created by the 1918 virus affected the lives of women, especially working-class women. This black comedy shows us how twin sisters, their sharp and shrewd mother, and many other women struggled to avoid being bitten by biters, cared gingerly for hunches who didn't want to eat their brains (just yet), and watched as the 'cured' lurkers started to take their jobs. Even during pandemics girls grow up, worry about boys, go out to work, get married, have babies, while striving to keep the brain safe inside the skull. At the beginning, the twins are small, fearful and helpless. At the end, they're armed and ready to go after the enemy – but who is the enemy?

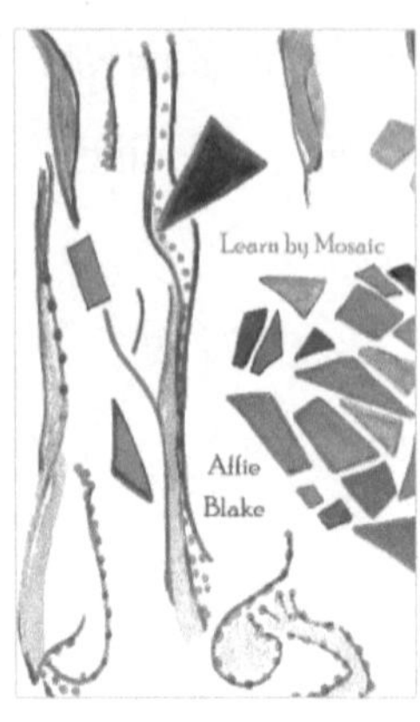

Learn by Mosaic

Affie Blake

ISBN: 978-1-7385926-5-4

127 x 203mm (5 x 8 in)

Page count: 192

Lil is a failure. A fait accompli of failure. She has failed in family, relationships, fashion, style, and employment. If failure were a skill, she would be a triumph, but it isn't, and she isn't. She is a failure.

Her dream of art and the artist life has diminished and her hope of eternal love, romance and a perfect relationship has faded, now in her late thirties, with, she feels, no marketable skills, or discernible talents teaching English is all she has. She could give an artist's impression of a good job but couldn't get one if her life depended upon it, and now she is beginning to feel it may well do. She can't understand how she seems to be a supporting actor in the movie of her own life and needs to do something with her life before life does something to her.

A light-hearted novel with bite, *Learn by Mosaic* is a relatable read and will resonate and stay with the reader long after they have finished reading the final page.